John H. Pratt, M.A.

A Treatise on Attractions, Laplace's Functions

And the Figure of the Earth John H. Pratt

John H. Pratt, M.A.

A Treatise on Attractions, Laplace's Functions
And the Figure of the Earth John H. Pratt

ISBN/EAN: 9783741192401

Manufactured in Europe, USA, Canada, Australia, Japa

Cover: Foto ©Andreas Hilbeck / pixelio.de

Manufactured and distributed by brebook publishing software
(www.brebook.com)

John H. Pratt, M.A.

A Treatise on Attractions, Laplace's Functions

A TREATISE ON

ATTRACTIONS, LAPLACE'S FUNCTIONS,

AND THE

FIGURE OF THE EARTH.

BY

JOHN H. PRATT, M.A.

ARCHDEACON OF CALCUTTA,

LATE FELLOW OF GONVILLE AND CAIUS COLLEGE, CAMBRIDGE, AND AUTHOR OF
"THE MATHEMATICAL PRINCIPLES OF MECHANICAL PHILOSOPHY."

SECOND EDITION.

Cambridge:
MACMILLAN AND CO.
AND 23, HENRIETTA STREET, COVENT GARDEN,
London.
1861.

Cambridge:

PRINTED BY C. J. CLAY, M.A.
AT THE UNIVERSITY PRESS.

PREFACE.

This Treatise is in part a republication of those portions of my work on *Mechanical Philosophy* which treat of Attractions, Laplace's Functions, and the Figure of the Earth.

The first edition, issued last year, consisted of a small number of copies. In the present issue the last Chapter has been rearranged and in part rewritten: other improvements have been made.

The disappearance of the *Mechanical Philosophy* has removed from the student—at any rate for the present, as no other work has yet appeared in English to supply the want—one subject of great importance and high interest, which that work first introduced into the University; I mean Laplace's Coefficients and Functions and the calculation of the Figure of the Earth by means of his remarkable analysis. The late Professor O'Brien subsequently published a Tract on the same subject; but it was incomplete. A Fourth Edition of Mr Airy's Tracts has been recently published, and in these is a treatise on the Figure of the Earth. But he adheres by choice (as stated in his Preface) to the "geometrical and quasi-geometrical methods." There is still room, therefore, for the present Treatise; as no student of the Higher Branches of Physical Astronomy should be ignorant of Laplace's Analysis and its results—"a calculus," to use Mr Airy's language, "the most singular in its nature, and the most powerful in its application that has ever appeared*."

There are problems in the Figure of the Earth which the geometric and quasi-geometric methods cannot touch, and of which the student must remain ignorant, if he is ignorant of the method of potentials.

It has been my endeavour to put the well-known difficulty in Laplace's analysis, arising from the use of a discontinuous function, in the clearest light, that the student may understand both what it is and how it is overcome. I have made use of Professor Stokes's valuable Paper in the Cambridge Philosophical Transactions of 1849 on the "Variation of Gravity at the surface of the Earth." I have also introduced some Propositions on the Geodetic Method of determining the Figure of the Earth, suggested by an acquaintance with the circumstances of the Great Trigonometrical Survey of India, and by the volume of the Ordnance Survey of Great Britain and Ireland recently published.

J. H. P.

CALCUTTA, 1861.

* See Article on *Figure of the Earth*, in the *Encyclopædia Metropolitana*, p. 191.

CONTENTS.

ATTRACTIONS AND LAPLACE'S FUNCTIONS.

CHAPTER I.

THE ATTRACTION OF SPHERICAL AND SPHEROIDAL BODIES.

CHAPTER II.

LAPLACE'S COEFFICIENTS AND FUNCTIONS.

CHAPTER III.

ATTRACTION OF BODIES NEARLY SPHERICAL.

CHAPTER IV.

ATTRACTION OF BODIES OF VARIOUS FORMS.

FIGURE OF THE EARTH.

CHAPTER I.

FIGURE OF THE EARTH, CONSIDERED AS A FLUID MASS, AND
THEREFORE CONSISTING OF STRATA NEARLY SPHERICAL.

CHAPTER II.

FIGURE OF THE EARTH, ON THE SOLE HYPOTHESIS OF THE
SURFACE BEING A SURFACE OF EQUILIBRIUM AND
NEARLY SPHERICAL.

CHAPTER III

THE FIGURE OF THE EARTH, DETERMINED BY GEODETIC OPERATIONS.

ATTRACTIONS AND LAPLACE'S FUNCTIONS.

1. THE Law of Universal Gravitation teaches us, that every particle of matter in the universe attracts every other particle of matter with a force varying directly as the mass of the attracting particle and inversely as the square of the distance between the attracted and the attracting particles. Taking this law as our basis of calculation, we shall investigate the amount of attraction exerted by spherical, spheroidal, and irregular nearly-spherical masses upon a particle, and apply our results in the second part of this Treatise to discover the Figure of the Earth. We shall also show how the attraction of irregular masses lying at the surface of the Earth may be estimated, in order afterwards to ascertain whether the irregularities of mountain-land and the ocean can have any effect on the calculation of this figure.

CHAPTER I.

ON THE ATTRACTION OF SPHERICAL AND SPHEROIDAL BODIES.

PROP. *To find the resultant attraction of an assemblage of particles constituting a homogeneous spherical shell of very small thickness upon a particle outside the shell: the law of attraction of the particles being that of the inverse square.*

2. Let O be the centre of the shell, P any particle of it, $OP = r$, dr the thickness, C the attracted particle, $\angle POC = \theta$; $mPMn$ a plane perpendicular to OC, ϕ the angle which the plane POC makes with the plane of the paper, $PC = y$.

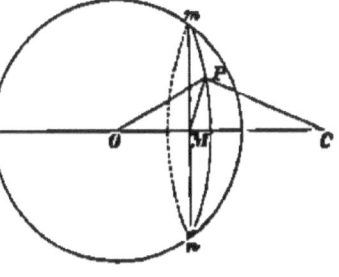

The attraction of the whole shell evidently acts in CO.

Let OP revolve about O through a small angle $d\theta$ in the plane MOP; then $r\,d\theta$ is the space described by P. Again, let OPM revolve about OC through a small angle $d\phi$, then $r\sin\theta\,d\phi$ is the space described by P. And the thickness of the shell is dr. Hence the volume of the elementary portion of the shell thus formed at P equals $r\,d\theta\,.\,r\sin\theta\,d\phi\,.\,dr$ ultimately, since its sides are ultimately at right angles to each other.

Then, if the unit of attraction be so chosen, that it equals the attraction of the unit of mass at the unit of distance, the attraction of the elementary mass at P on C in the direction CP

$$= \frac{\rho r^2 \sin\theta\, dr d\theta d\phi}{y^2}\,,\ \rho \text{ the density of the shell;}$$

$\therefore$ attraction of P on C in $CO = \dfrac{\rho r^2 \sin\theta\, dr d\theta d\phi}{y^2}\dfrac{c-r\cos\theta}{y}.$

We shall eliminate θ from this equation by means of

$$y^2 = c^2 + r^2 - 2cr\cos\theta,$$

$$\therefore \sin\theta\frac{d\theta}{dy} = \frac{y}{cr},\ \ c - r\cos\theta = \frac{y^2 + c^2 - r^2}{2c};$$

$\therefore$ attraction of P on C in $CO = \dfrac{\rho r\, dr}{2c^2}\left(1 + \dfrac{c^2 - r^2}{y^2}\right)dy\,d\phi.$

To obtain the attraction of all the particles of the shell we integrate this with respect to ϕ and y, the limits of ϕ being 0 and 2π, those of y being $c - r$ and $c + r$;

$\therefore$ attraction of shell on $C = \dfrac{\rho r\, dr}{2c^2}\displaystyle\int_{c-r}^{c+r}\int_0^{2\pi}\left(1 + \dfrac{c^2 - r^2}{y^2}\right)dy\,d\phi$

$$= \frac{\pi\rho r\, dr}{c^2}\int_{c-r}^{c+r}\left(1 + \frac{c^2 - r^2}{y^2}\right)dy = \frac{\pi\rho r\, dr}{c^2}\,(2r + 2r)$$

$$= \frac{4\pi\rho r^2 dr}{c^2} = \frac{\text{mass of shell}}{c^2}\,.$$

This result shows that the shell attracts the particle at C in the same manner as if the mass of the shell were condensed into its centre.

3. It follows also that a sphere, which is either homogeneous or consists of concentric spherical shells of uniform density, will attract the particle C in the same manner as if the whole mass were collected at its centre.

PROP. *To find the attraction of a homogeneous spherical shell of small thickness on a particle situated within it.*

4. We must proceed as in the last Proposition; but the limits of y are in this case $r - c$ and $r + c$; hence,

$$\text{attraction of shell} = \frac{\pi \rho r dr}{c^2} \int_{r-c}^{r+c} \left(1 - \frac{r^2 - c^2}{y^2}\right) dy$$

$$= \frac{\pi \rho r dr}{c^2} (2c - 2c) = 0 ;$$

therefore the particle within the shell is equally attracted in every direction.

5. This result may easily be arrived at geometrically in the following manner. Through the attracted point suppose an elementary double cone to be drawn, cutting the shell in two places. The inclinations of the elementary portions of the shell, thus cut out, to the axis of the cone will be the same, the thickness the same, but the other two dimensions of the elements will each vary as the distance from the attracted point; and therefore the masses of the two opposite elements of the shell will vary directly as the square of the distance from that point, and consequently their attractions will be exactly equal, and being in opposite directions will not affect the point. The whole shell may be thus divided into pairs of equal attracting elements and in opposite directions, and therefore the whole shell has no effect in drawing the point in any one direction more than in another.

6. The results of these two Propositions are so simple and beautiful, that it is interesting to enquire whether these

properties belong exclusively or not to the law of the inverse square of the distance. To determine this is the object of the four following Propositions.

PROP. *To find the attraction of a homogeneous spherical shell on a particle without it; the law of attraction being represented by* $\phi(y)$, *y being the distance.*

7. The calculation is exactly analogous to that given above: we have only to alter the law of attraction. Then attraction on C in CO .

$$= \frac{\pi \rho r dr}{c^2} \int_{c-r}^{c+r} (y^2 + c^2 - r^2)\, \phi(y)\, dy \text{ (integrated by parts)}$$

$$= \frac{\pi \rho r dr}{c^2} [(y^2 + c^2 - r^2) \int \phi(y)\, dy - 2\int \{y \int \phi(y)\, dy\}\, dy]$$

$$= \frac{\pi \rho r dr}{c^2} \{(y^2 + c^2 - r^2)\, \phi_1(y) - 2\psi(y) + \text{const.}\} \text{ suppose,}$$

$$= 2\pi \rho r dr \left\{ \frac{c+r}{c} \phi_1(c+r) - \frac{1}{c^3}\psi(c+r) - \frac{c-r}{c}\phi_1(c-r) + \frac{1}{c^3}\psi(c-r) \right\}$$

$$= 2\pi \rho r dr \frac{d}{dc} \left\{ \frac{\psi(c+r) - \psi(c-r)}{c} \right\},$$

this latter form being introduced merely as an analytical artifice to simplify the expression.

PROP. *To find the attraction of the shell on an internal particle, with the same law.*

8. The calculation is the same as in the last Article, except that the limits of y are $r - c$ and $r + c$:

$$\therefore \text{ attraction} = 2\pi \rho r dr \left\{ \frac{r+c}{c}\phi_1(r+c) - \frac{1}{c^3}\psi(r+c) \right.$$

$$\left. + \frac{r-c}{c}\phi_1(r-c) + \frac{1}{c^3}\psi(r-c) \right\}$$

$$= 2\pi \rho r dr \frac{d}{dc} \left\{ \frac{\psi(r+c) - \psi(r-c)}{c} \right\}.$$

PROP. *To find what laws of attraction allow us to suppose a spherical shell condensed into its centre when attracting an external point.*

9. Let $\phi(r)$ be the law of force; then if c be the distance of the centre of the shell from the attracted point and r the radius of the shell, and

$$\psi(r) = \int \{r \int \phi(r)\, dr\}\, dr,$$

then the attraction of the shell

$$= 2\pi \rho r\, dr\, \frac{d}{dc}\left\{ \frac{\psi(c+r) - \psi(c-r)}{c} \right\}.$$

But if the shell be condensed into its centre, the attraction

$$= 4\pi \rho r^2\, dr\, \phi(c);$$

$$\therefore\ 2r\phi(c) = \frac{d}{dc}\left\{ \frac{\psi(c+r) - \psi(c-r)}{c} \right\}$$

$$= 2\frac{d}{dc}\left(\frac{d\psi c}{dc}\frac{r}{c} + \frac{d^3\psi c}{dc^3}\frac{r^3}{c}\frac{1}{1.2.3} + \dots \right)$$

$$= 2r\phi(c) + 2\frac{d}{dc}\left(\frac{d^3\psi c}{dc^3}\frac{r^3}{c}\frac{1}{1.2.3} + \dots \right);$$

$$\therefore\ \frac{d}{dc}\left(\frac{1}{c}\frac{d^3\psi c}{dc^3} + \dots \right) = 0,\ \text{whatever } r \text{ be};$$

$$\therefore\ \frac{d}{dc}\left(\frac{1}{c}\frac{d^3\psi c}{dc^3} \right) = 0,\quad \frac{d}{dc}\left(\frac{1}{c}\frac{d^5\psi c}{dc^5} \right) = 0,\ \dots$$

But $\dfrac{d\psi c}{dc} = c\int \phi(c)\, dc,\quad \dfrac{d^2\psi c}{dc^2} = \int \phi(c)\, dc + c\phi(c),$

$$\frac{d^3\psi c}{dc^3} = 2\phi c + c\frac{d\phi c}{dc};$$

therefore by the first of the above equations of condition

$$\frac{2}{c}\phi c + \frac{d\phi c}{dc} = \text{const.} = 3A,$$

and multiplying by c^2 and integrating

$$c^2 \phi(c) = Ac^2 + B,$$

A and B being independent of c,

$$\phi(c) = Ac + \frac{B}{c^3}.$$

This is the most general solution of the first of the equations of condition for $\psi(c)$, and it satisfies all the rest. Hence the only laws of attraction which have the property in question are those of the direct distance, the inverse square, and a law compounded of these.

PROP. *To find for what laws the shell attracts an internal point equally in every direction.*

10.   When this is the case

$$\frac{d}{dc}\left\{\frac{\psi(r+c) - \psi(r-c)}{c}\right\} = 0,$$

$$\frac{d\psi r}{dr} + \frac{d^3\psi r}{dr^3}\frac{c^2}{1.2.3} + \ldots = -A,$$

whatever c is, A being a constant independent of c;

$$\therefore \frac{d\psi r}{dr} = -A, \quad \frac{d^3\psi r}{dr^3} = 0, \ldots$$

These conditions are all satisfied if the first is: this gives

$$r \int \phi(r)\, dr = -A, \quad \phi(r) = \frac{A}{r^2},$$

and therefore the inverse square is the only law which possesses this property.

11.   The form of the Earth and of the other bodies of the Solar System differing from the spherical, and more resembling the spheroidal, it is desirable to find the attraction of a spheroid upon an external and an internal point.

PROP. *To find the attraction of a homogeneous oblate spheroid upon a particle within its mass; the law of attraction being that of the inverse square of the distance.*

12. Let a, c be the semi-axes; the minor axis $2c$ coinciding with the axis of z: then the equation to the spheroid from the centre is

$$\frac{x^2 + y^2}{a^2} + \frac{z^2}{c^2} = 1.$$

Let fgh be the co-ordinates to the attracted particle, which we shall take as the origin of polar co-ordinates,

$r =$ radius vector of any particle of the attracting mass,

$\theta =$ angle which r makes with a line parallel to z,

$\phi =$ angle which the plane in which θ is measured makes with the plane xz;

$$\therefore \ x = f + r \sin\theta \cos\phi, \quad y = g + r \sin\theta \sin\phi, \quad z = h + r \cos\theta,$$

and the equation to the spheroid becomes

$$\frac{(f + r\sin\theta\cos\phi)^2 + (g + r\sin\theta\sin\phi)^2}{a^2} + \frac{(h + r\cos\theta)^2}{c^2} = 1,$$

or $r^2 \left(\dfrac{\sin^2\theta}{a^2} + \dfrac{\cos^2\theta}{c^2} \right) + 2r \left(\dfrac{f\sin\theta\cos\phi + g\sin\theta\sin\phi}{a^2} + \dfrac{h\cos\theta}{c^2} \right)$

$$= 1 - \frac{f^2 + g^2}{a^2} - \frac{h^2}{c^2};$$

put $\dfrac{\sin^2\theta}{a^2} + \dfrac{\cos^2\theta}{c^2} = K,$

$$\frac{f\sin\theta\cos\phi + g\sin\theta\sin\phi}{a^2} + \frac{h\cos\theta}{c^2} = F,$$

and $\quad F^2 + K \left(1 - \dfrac{f^2 + g^2}{a^2} - \dfrac{h^2}{c^2} \right) = H,$

then $\quad K^2 r^2 + 2KFr + F^2 = H,$

and the values of r are

$$r' = \frac{-F + \sqrt{(H)}}{K} \quad \text{and} \quad r'' = \frac{-F - \sqrt{(H)}}{K}.$$

The volume of the attracting element $= r^2 \sin\theta \, dr \, d\theta \, d\phi$ as in Art. 2: let ρ be the density of the spheroid. Then the attraction of this element on the attracted particle is

$$\rho \sin\theta \, dr \, d\theta \, d\phi:$$

and the resolved parts of this parallel to the axes of xyz are

$$\rho \sin^2\theta \cos\phi \, dr \, d\theta \, d\phi, \quad \rho \sin^2\theta \sin\phi \, dr \, d\theta \, d\phi,$$

$$\rho \sin\theta \cos\theta \, dr \, d\theta \, d\phi.$$

Let A, B, C be the attractions of the whole spheroid in the directions of the axes, estimated positive towards the centre of the spheroid. Then these equal the integrals of the attractions of the element; the limits of r being $-r'$ and r'', of θ being 0 and π, of ϕ being 0 and π. Hence

$$A = -\int_{-r'}^{r''}\int_0^\pi\int_0^\pi \rho \sin^2\theta \cos\phi \, dr \, d\theta \, d\phi,$$

$$B = -\int_{-r'}^{r''}\int_0^\pi\int_0^\pi \rho \sin^2\theta \sin\phi \, dr \, d\theta \, d\phi,$$

$$C = -\int_{-r'}^{r''}\int_0^\pi\int_0^\pi \rho \sin\theta \cos\theta \, dr \, d\theta \, d\phi,$$

$$A = -\rho\int_0^\pi\int_0^\pi (r'' + r') \sin^2\theta \cos\phi \, d\theta \, d\phi$$

$$= 2\rho\int_0^\pi\int_0^\pi \frac{F}{K} \sin^2\theta \cos\phi \, d\theta \, d\phi.$$

Now it is easily seen that if $R(\sin\alpha, \cos^2\alpha)$ be a rational function of $\sin\alpha$ and $\cos^2\alpha$, then

$$\int_0^\pi R(\sin\alpha, \cos^2\alpha) \cos\alpha \, d\alpha = 0.$$

Therefore by substituting for F and K we have

$$A = 2 f \rho c^2 \int_0^\pi\int_0^\pi \frac{\sin^2\theta \cos^2\phi \, d\theta \, d\phi}{c^2 \sin^2\theta + a^2 \cos^2\theta}$$

$$= \pi f \rho c^2 \int_0^\pi \frac{\sin^3 \theta\, d\theta}{c^2 \sin^2\theta + a^2 \cos^2\theta} = \pi f \rho c^2 \int_0^\pi \frac{(1-\cos^2\theta)\sin\theta\, d\theta}{c^2 + (a^2 - c^2)\cos^2\theta} *$$

$$= \pi f \rho \frac{c^2}{a^2 - c^2} \int_0^\pi \left\{ \frac{a^2 \sin\theta}{c^2 + (a^2 - c^2)\cos^2\theta} - \sin\theta \right\} d\theta$$

$$= \pi f \rho \frac{c^2}{a^2 - c^2} \left\{ -\frac{a^2}{c\sqrt{a^2 - c^2}} \tan^{-1}\left(\frac{\sqrt{a^2 - c^2}}{c}\cos\theta \right) + \cos\theta + \text{const.} \right\}$$

$$= 2\pi f \rho \frac{c^2}{a^2 - c^2} \left\{ \frac{a^2}{c\sqrt{a^2 - c^2}} \tan^{-1}\frac{\sqrt{a^2 - c^2}}{c} - 1 \right\}, \quad \frac{c^2}{a^2} = 1 - e^2,$$

$$= 2\pi f \rho \left\{ \frac{\sqrt{1-e^2}}{e^2} \tan^{-1}\frac{e}{\sqrt{1-e^2}} - \frac{1-e^2}{e^2} \right\}$$

$$= 2\pi f \rho \left\{ \frac{\sqrt{1-e^2}}{e^3} \sin^{-1} e - \frac{1-e^2}{e^2} \right\}.$$

In the same manner we should find that

$$B = 2\pi g \rho \left\{ \frac{\sqrt{1-e^2}}{e^3} \sin^{-1} e - \frac{1-e^2}{e^2} \right\}.$$

Also $\quad C = 2\rho \int_0^\pi \int_0^\pi \frac{F}{K} \sin\theta \cos\theta\, d\theta\, d\phi$

$$= 2\rho h a^2 \int_0^\pi \int_0^\pi \frac{\sin\theta \cos^2\theta\, d\theta\, d\phi}{c^2 \sin^2\theta + a^2 \cos^2\theta}$$

$$= 2\pi \rho h \frac{a^2}{a^2 - c^2} \int_0^\pi \left\{ \sin\theta - \frac{c^2 \sin\theta}{c^2 + (a^2 - c^2)\cos^2\theta} \right\} d\theta$$

$$= 4\pi \rho h \frac{a^2}{a^2 - c^2} \left\{ 1 - \frac{c}{\sqrt{a^2 - c^2}} \tan^{-1}\frac{\sqrt{a^2 - c^2}}{c} \right\}$$

$$= 4\pi \rho h \left\{ \frac{1}{e^2} - \frac{\sqrt{1-e^2}}{e^3} \sin^{-1} e \right\}.$$

* If the spheroid be prolate, c is $> a$ and the denominator of this must be written $c^2 - (c^2 - a^2)\cos^2\theta$, and the integral would involve logarithms instead of circular arcs.

13. We gather from these expressions, that the attraction is independent of the magnitude of the spheroid, and depends solely upon its ellipticity. Hence the attraction of the spheroid similar to the given one, and passing through the attracted particle, is the same as that of any other similar concentric spheroid comprising the attracted particle in its mass. Hence a spheroidal shell, the surfaces of which are similar and concentric, attracts a point within it equally in all directions. This property can be proved geometrically exactly as in Art. 5.

14. If we put the ellipticity of the spheroid $= \epsilon$, and suppose ϵ so small that we may neglect its square, we have

$$e^2 = 1 - \frac{c^2}{a^2} = 1 - (1 - \epsilon)^2 = 2\epsilon ;$$

$$\therefore A = \frac{4}{3} \pi \rho \left(1 - \frac{2}{5} \epsilon \right) f, \quad B = \frac{4}{3} \pi \rho \left(1 - \frac{2}{5} \epsilon \right) g,$$

$$C = \frac{4}{3} \pi \rho \left(1 + \frac{4}{5} \epsilon \right) h.$$

If we had taken an ellipsoid instead of a spheroid, the expressions would not have been capable of integration.

15. If we had attempted to find the attraction on an external particle according to the process of the last Article, we should have fallen upon expressions which no known methods have yet integrated: and therefore we are unable by any direct means to obtain the attraction of a spheroid on an external particle. Mr Ivory has, however, devised an indirect method of obtaining it, which we shall now proceed to develop. He has discovered a theorem by which the attraction of an ellipsoid upon an external particle is shown to be proportional to that of another ellipsoid, dependent on the first for form and dimensions, upon a particle internal to it, and therefore (in the case of a spheroid, or ellipsoid of revolution) determinable by the last Proposition.

PROP. *To enunciate and prove Ivory's Theorem.*

16. Let $\frac{x^2}{a^2} + \frac{y^2}{b^2} + \frac{z^2}{c^2} = 1$, and $\frac{x^2}{a^2} + \frac{y^2}{\beta^2} + \frac{z^2}{\gamma^2} = 1$,

be the equations to the surfaces of two ellipsoids having the same centre and foci: then

$$a^2 - b^2 = a^2 - \beta^2, \quad a^2 - c^2 = a^2 - \gamma^2 \dots\dots\dots (1).$$

Let fgh, $f'g'h'$ be the co-ordinates to two particles so situated on the surfaces of these ellipsoids that

$$\frac{f}{f'} = \frac{a}{a'}, \quad \frac{g}{g'} = \frac{b}{\beta}, \quad \frac{h}{h'} = \frac{c}{\gamma} \dots\dots\dots\dots (2).$$

Also since $(fgh)(f'g'h')$ are points in the surfaces of the first and second ellipsoids respectively, we have

$$\frac{f^2}{a^2} + \frac{g^2}{b^2} + \frac{h^2}{c^2} = 1, \quad \frac{f'^2}{a^2} + \frac{g'^2}{\beta^2} + \frac{h'^2}{\gamma^2} = 1 \dots\dots\dots (3).$$

Then the attraction of the first ellipsoid parallel to the axis of x on the particle at the point $(f'g'h')$ on the surface of the second, is to the attraction of the second ellipsoid on the particle at the point (fgh) on the surface of the first in the same direction, as ab : aβ, the law of attraction being any function of the distance: and similarly with respect to the axes of y and z. This is Ivory's Theorem.

We shall, for convenience, represent the law of attraction by the function $r\phi(r^2)$, r being the distance.

The attraction of the first ellipsoid on the particle $(f'g'h')$ parallel to the axis of z

$$= \rho\iiint (h' - z)\, \phi\, \{(f' - x)^2 + (g' - y)^2 + (h' - z)^2\}\, dx\, dy\, dz,$$

the limits of z are $-c\sqrt{\left(1 - \frac{x^2}{a^2} - \frac{y^2}{b^2}\right)}$, and $c\sqrt{\left(1 - \frac{x^2}{a^2} - \frac{y^2}{b^2}\right)}$,

the limits of y are $-b\sqrt{\left(1 - \frac{x^2}{a^2}\right)}$, and $b\sqrt{\left(1 - \frac{x^2}{a^2}\right)}$,

and the limits of x are $-a$ and a

$$= \rho\iint [\psi\, \{(f' - x)^2 + (g' - y)^2 + (h' + z)^2\}$$
$$- \psi\, \{(f' - x)^2 + (g' - y)^2 + (h' - z)^2\}]\, dx\, dy$$

between the specified limits:

$$\psi(r) = \frac{1}{2} \int \phi(r) \, dr :$$

it must be remembered that in this expression

$$z = c \sqrt{\left(1 - \frac{x^2}{a^2} - \frac{y^2}{b^2}\right)},$$

but we do not substitute this value merely that the function may be preserved under as simple a form as possible. Now put $x = ar$, $y = bs$, $z = ct$, then the attraction

$$= \rho ab \iint [\psi \,[(f' - ar)^2 + (g' - bs)^2 + (h' - ct)^2]$$
$$- \psi \,[(f' - ar)^2 + (g' - bs)^2 + (h' + ct)^2]] \, dr \, ds,$$

the limits of s being $-\sqrt{(1 - r^2)}$ and $\sqrt{(1 - r^2)}$, and those of r being -1 and 1: also $t = \sqrt{(1 - r^2 - s^2)}$.

Now $(f' - ar)^2 + (g' - bs)^2 + (h' \pm ct)^2$

$$= f'^2 + g'^2 + h'^2 - 2 (f'ar + g'bs \pm h'ct) + a^2r^2 + b^2s^2 + c^2t^2,$$

substituting for h'^2 by (3) and for t^2,

$$= f'^2 \left(1 - \frac{\gamma^2}{a^2}\right) + g'^2 \left(1 - \frac{\gamma^2}{\beta^2}\right) + \gamma^2 - 2 (f'ar + g'bs \pm h'ct)$$
$$+ (a^2 - c^2) \, r^2 + (b^2 - c^2) \, s^2 + c^2,$$

eliminating $f'g'h'$ by (2) and making use of (1),

$$= \frac{f^2}{a^2} (a^2 - c^2) + \frac{g^2}{\beta^2} (b^2 - c^2) + c^2 - 2 (f ar + g \beta s \pm h \gamma t)$$
$$+ (a^2 - \gamma^2) \, r^2 + (\beta^2 - \gamma^2) \, s^2 + \gamma^2$$

$$= f^2 + g^2 + h^2 - 2 (f ar + g \beta s \pm h \gamma t) + a^2 r^2 + \beta^2 s^2 + \gamma^2 t^2, \text{ by (3)},$$

$$= (f - ar)^2 + (g - \beta s)^2 + (h \pm \gamma t).$$

Hence the attraction of the First Ellipsoid on $(f'g'h')$ parallel to z,

$$= \rho ab \iint [\psi \,[(f - ar)^2 + (g - \beta s)^2 + (h + \gamma t)^2]$$
$$- \psi \,[(f - ar)^2 + (g - \beta s)^2 + (h - \gamma t)^2]] \, dr \, ds$$

$$= \frac{ab}{\alpha\beta} \times \text{ attraction of Second Ellipsoid on } (fgh) \text{ in the same}$$

direction.

The same may be proved for the attractions parallel to the other axes: and consequently the Theorem, as enunciated, is true.

We may observe that one of these ellipsoids must necessarily be wholly within the other. For if not, the points in which they cut each other lie in the line of which the equations are

$$\frac{x^2}{a^2} + \frac{y^2}{b^2} + \frac{z^2}{c^2} = 1 \quad \text{and} \quad \frac{x^2}{\alpha^2} + \frac{y^2}{\beta^2} + \frac{z^2}{\gamma^2} = 1.$$

Suppose a less than α; the points of intersection must satisfy the equation

$$x^2 \left(\frac{1}{a^2} - \frac{1}{\alpha^2} \right) + y^2 \left(\frac{1}{b^2} - \frac{1}{\beta^2} \right) + z^2 \left(\frac{1}{c^2} - \frac{1}{\gamma^2} \right) = 0;$$

and this by (1) becomes

$$\left(\frac{x}{a\alpha} \right)^2 + \left(\frac{y}{b\beta} \right)^2 + \left(\frac{z}{c\gamma} \right)^2 = 0,$$

an equation which can be satisfied only by $x = 0$, $y = 0$, $z = 0$. But these do not satisfy the equations above; and therefore the surfaces do not intersect in any point.

To find the attraction of any ellipsoid of which the semi-axes are a, b, c upon an external point $(f'g'h')$ by the help of this Theorem, we must first calculate the attraction of an ellipsoid of which the semi-axes are $\alpha\beta\gamma$, determined by equations (1) and the second of (3), on an internal point (fgh), f, g and h being given by equations (2). And then the attractions required will be those multiplied by

$$\frac{bc}{\beta\gamma}, \quad \frac{ac}{\alpha\gamma}, \quad \frac{ab}{\alpha\beta}, \quad \text{respectively.}$$

CHAPTER II.

17. In the present Chapter we shall develop the properties of those remarkable quantities which have received the name of their great discoverer, under the designation of LAPLACE'S COEFFICIENTS AND FUNCTIONS. To do this it will be necessary to anticipate the subject of the following Chapter, and to bring in here a Proposition which should properly stand at the head of that division of this treatise.

PROP. *To obtain formulæ for the calculation of the attraction of a heterogeneous mass upon any particle.*

18. Let ρ be the density of the body at the point (xyz); fgh the co-ordinates of the attracted particle; and, as before, suppose that A, B, C are the attractions parallel to the axes x, y, z. Then

$$A = \iiint \frac{\rho\,(f-x)\,dx\,dy\,dz}{[(f-x)^2 + (g-y)^2 + (h-z)^2]^{\frac{3}{2}}},$$

$$B = \iiint \frac{\rho\,(g-y)\,dx\,dy\,dz}{[(f-x)^2 + (g-y)^2 + (h-z)^2]^{\frac{3}{2}}},$$

$$C = \iiint \frac{\rho\,(h-z)\,dx\,dy\,dz}{[(f-x)^2 + (g-y)^2 + (h-z)^2]^{\frac{3}{2}}},$$

the limits being determined by the equation to the surface of the body.

Let $$V = \iiint \frac{\rho\,dx\,dy\,dz}{[(f-x)^2 + (g-y)^2 + (h-z)^2]^{\frac{1}{2}}};$$

$$\therefore A = -\frac{dV}{df}, \quad B = -\frac{dV}{dg}, \quad C = -\frac{dV}{dh}.$$

19. It follows, then, that the calculation of the attractions A, B, C depends upon that of V. This function cannot be calculated except when expanded into a series. It is a function of great importance in Physics: and, for the sake of a name, has been denominated the *Potential* of the attracting mass, as upon its value the amount of the attractive force of the body depends.

20. As the axes and origin of co-ordinates in the previous Article are altogether arbitrary, it follows that if r be the distance of the attracted point from any fixed point in the attracting body, then the attraction in the line of r, towards the origin of r, $= -\dfrac{dV}{dr}$.

PROP. *To prove that* $\dfrac{d^2V}{df^2} + \dfrac{d^2V}{dg^2} + \dfrac{d^2V}{dh^2} = 0$, *or* $-4\pi\rho'$, *according as the attracted particle is not or is part of the mass itself;* ρ' *being the density of the attracted particle in the latter case.*

21. By differentiating V, we have

$$\frac{dV}{df} = \iiint \frac{-\rho\,(f-x)\,dx\,dy\,dz}{\{(f-x)^2 + (g-y)^2 + (h-z)^2\}^{\frac{3}{2}}},$$

$$\frac{d^2V}{df^2} = \iiint \frac{\rho\,[2\,(f-x)^2 - (g-y)^2 - (h-z)^2]\,dx\,dy\,dz}{\{(f-x)^2 + (g-y)^2 + (h-z)^2\}^{\frac{5}{2}}}.$$

In the same manner we shall have

$$\frac{d^2V}{dg^2} = \iiint \frac{\rho\,[2\,(g-y)^2 - (f-x)^2 - (h-z)^2]\,dx\,dy\,dz}{\{(f-x)^2 + (g-y)^2 + (h-z)^2\}^{\frac{5}{2}}},$$

$$\frac{d^2V}{dh^2} = \iiint \frac{\rho\,[2\,(h-z)^2 - (f-x)^2 - (g-y)^2]\,dx\,dy\,dz}{\{(f-x)^2 + (g-y)^2 + (h-z)^2\}^{\frac{5}{2}}};$$

$$\therefore \frac{d^2V}{df^2} + \frac{d^2V}{dg^2} + \frac{d^2V}{dh^2} = \iiint \frac{0 \times dx\,dy\,dz}{\{(f-x)^2 + (g-y)^2 + (h-z)^2\}^{\frac{3}{2}}}.$$

When the attracted particle is not a portion of the attracting mass itself, then xyz will never equal fgh respectively, and consequently the expression under the signs of integration vanishes for every particle of the mass :

$$\therefore \; \frac{d^2V}{df^2} + \frac{d^2V}{dg^2} + \frac{d^2V}{dh^2} = 0.$$

This equation was first given by Laplace: and Poisson was the first who showed that it is not true when the attracted particle is part of the attracting mass. In that case the denominator of the fraction under the signs of integration vanishes, and the fraction becomes $\frac{0}{0}$, when $x = f$, $y = g$, $z = h$.

To determine the value of $\frac{d^2V}{df^2} + \frac{d^2V}{dg^2} + \frac{d^2V}{dh^2}$ in that case, suppose a sphere described in the body, so that it shall include the attracted particle; and let $V = U + U'$, U referring to the sphere, and U' to the excess of the body over the sphere. Then, by what is already proved,

$$\frac{d^2U'}{df^2} + \frac{d^2U'}{dg^2} + \frac{d^2U'}{dh^2} = 0;$$

$$\therefore \; \frac{d^2V}{df^2} + \frac{d^2V}{dg^2} + \frac{d^2V}{dh^2} = \frac{d^2U}{df^2} + \frac{d^2U}{dg^2} + \frac{d^2U}{dh^2}.$$

The centre of the sphere may be chosen as near the attracted particle as we please; and therefore the radius of the sphere may be taken so small that its density may be considered uniform and equal to that at the point (fgh), which we shall call ρ'.

Let $f'g'h'$ be the co-ordinates to the centre of the sphere; then the attractions of the sphere on the attracted point parallel to the axes are, by Art. 3,

$$\frac{4\pi\rho'}{3}(f-f'), \quad \frac{4\pi\rho'}{3}(g-g'), \quad \frac{4\pi\rho'}{3}(h-h'),$$

or $-\dfrac{dU}{df}, \quad -\dfrac{dU}{dg}, \quad -\dfrac{dU}{dh}$, by Art. 20.

$$\therefore \frac{d^2U}{df^2} + \frac{d^2U}{dg^2} + \frac{d^2U}{dh^2} = -4\pi\rho';$$

$$\therefore \frac{d^2V}{df^2} + \frac{d^2V}{dg^2} + \frac{d^2V}{dh^2} = -4\pi\rho',$$

when the attracted particle is within the attracting mass.

22. It may be shown by precisely the same process as in the previous Article, that

$$\frac{d^2R}{df^2} + \frac{d^2R}{dg^2} + \frac{d^2R}{dh^2} = 0,$$

where $R = [(f-x)^2 + (g-y)^2 + (h-z)^2]^{-\frac{1}{2}}$,

the reciprocal of the distance of any point of the body from the attracted particle.

PROP. *To transform the partial differential equation in R into polar co-ordinates.*

23. Let $r\theta\omega$ be the co-ordinates of (fgh), and $r'\theta'\omega'$ of (xyz), the angles θ and θ' being measured from the axis of z; ω and ω' being the angles which the planes on which θ and θ' are measured make with the plane zx. Then

$$f = r\sin\theta\cos\omega, \quad g = r\sin\theta\sin\omega, \quad h = r\cos\theta,$$

$$x = r'\sin\theta'\cos\omega', \quad g' = r'\sin\theta'\sin\omega', \quad h' = r'\cos\theta'.$$

These are the same as

$$r^2 = f^2 + g^2 + h^2, \quad \cos\theta = \frac{h}{\sqrt{f^2+g^2+h^2}}, \quad \tan\omega = \frac{g}{f} \quad \ldots\ldots (1) ;$$

$$\therefore \frac{dR}{df} = \frac{dR}{dr}\frac{dr}{df} + \frac{dR}{d\theta}\frac{d\theta}{df} + \frac{dR}{d\omega}\frac{d\omega}{df},$$

$$\frac{d^2R}{df^2} = \frac{d}{df}\frac{dR}{dr}\frac{dr}{df} + \frac{d}{df}\frac{dR}{d\theta}\frac{d\theta}{df} + \frac{d}{df}\frac{dR}{d\omega}\frac{d\omega}{df}$$

$$+ \frac{dR}{dr}\frac{d^2r}{df^2} + \frac{dR}{d\theta}\frac{d^2\theta}{df^2} + \frac{dR}{d\omega}\frac{d^2\omega}{df^2}$$

$$= \frac{d^2R}{dr^2}\frac{dr^2}{df^2} + \frac{d^2R}{d\theta^2}\frac{d\theta^2}{df^2} + \frac{d^2R}{d\omega^2}\frac{d\omega^2}{df^2}$$

$$+ 2\frac{d^2R}{dr\,d\theta}\frac{dr}{df}\frac{d\theta}{df} + 2\frac{d^2R}{dr\,d\omega}\frac{dr}{df}\frac{d\omega}{df} + 2\frac{d^2R}{d\theta\,d\omega}\frac{d\theta}{df}\frac{d\omega}{df}$$

$$+ \frac{dR}{dr}\frac{d^2r}{df^2} + \frac{dR}{d\theta}\frac{d^2\theta}{df^2} + \frac{dR}{d\omega}\frac{d^2\omega}{df^2}.$$

The expressions for $\frac{d^2R}{dg^2}$ and $\frac{d^2R}{dh^2}$ are of the same form. These three must be added together and equated to zero. When this is effected the formulæ (1) make

the coefficient of $\dfrac{d^2R}{dr^2} = \dfrac{dr^2}{df^2} + \dfrac{dr^2}{dg^2} + \dfrac{dr^2}{dh^2} = 1,$

the coefficient of $\dfrac{d^2R}{d\theta^2} = \dfrac{d\theta^2}{df^2} + \dfrac{d\theta^2}{dg^2} + \dfrac{d\theta^2}{dh^2} = \dfrac{1}{r^2},$

the coefficient of $\dfrac{d^2R}{d\omega^2} = \dfrac{d\omega^2}{df^2} + \dfrac{d\omega^2}{dg^2} + \dfrac{d\omega^2}{dh^2} = \dfrac{1}{r^2\sin^2\theta},$

the coefficient of $\dfrac{d^2R}{dr\,d\theta} = 2\dfrac{dr}{df}\dfrac{d\theta}{df} + 2\dfrac{dr}{dg}\dfrac{d\theta}{dg} + 2\dfrac{dr}{dh}\dfrac{d\theta}{dh} = 0,$

the coefficient of $\dfrac{d^2R}{dr\,d\omega} = 2\dfrac{dr}{df}\dfrac{d\omega}{df} + 2\dfrac{dr}{dg}\dfrac{d\omega}{dg} + 2\dfrac{dr}{dh}\dfrac{d\omega}{dh} = 0,$

the coefficient of $\dfrac{d^2R}{d\theta\,d\omega} = 2\dfrac{d\theta}{df}\dfrac{d\omega}{df} + 2\dfrac{d\theta}{dg}\dfrac{d\omega}{dg} + 2\dfrac{d\theta}{dh}\dfrac{d\omega}{dh} = 0,$

the coefficient of $\dfrac{dR}{dr} = \dfrac{d^2r}{df^2} + \dfrac{d^2r}{dg^2} + \dfrac{d^2r}{dh^2} = \dfrac{2}{r},$

the coefficient of $\dfrac{dR}{d\theta} = \dfrac{d^2\theta}{df^2} + \dfrac{d^2\theta}{dg^2} + \dfrac{d^2\theta}{dh^2} = \dfrac{\cos\theta}{r^2\sin\theta},$

the coefficient of $\dfrac{dR}{d\omega} = \dfrac{d^2\omega}{df^2} + \dfrac{d^2\omega}{dg^2} + \dfrac{d^2\omega}{dh^2} = 0.$

Hence the equation in R becomes

$$\frac{d^2R}{dr^2} + \frac{2}{r}\frac{dR}{dr} + \frac{1}{r^2}\frac{d^2R}{d\theta^2} + \frac{\cos\theta}{r^2\sin\theta}\frac{dR}{d\theta} + \frac{1}{r^2\sin^2\theta}\frac{d^2R}{d\omega^2} = 0;$$

$$\therefore r\frac{d^2.rR}{dr^2} + \frac{d^2R}{d\theta^2} + \frac{\cos\theta}{\sin\theta}\frac{dR}{d\theta} + \frac{1}{\sin^2\theta}\frac{d^2R}{d\omega^2} = 0.$$

Put $\cos\theta = \mu$, then

$$r\frac{d^2.rR}{dr^2} + \frac{d}{d\mu}\left\{(1-\mu^2)\frac{dR}{d\mu}\right\} + \frac{1}{1-\mu^2}\frac{d^2R}{d\omega^2} = 0.$$

PROP. *To explain the method of expanding R in a series.*

24. The expression for R becomes, when the polar co-ordinates are substituted,

$$[r^2 + r'^2 - 2rr'\,[\mu\mu' + \sqrt{1-\mu^2}\sqrt{1-\mu'^2}\cos(\omega - \omega')]]^{-1},$$

and this may be expanded into either of the series

$$\left.\begin{array}{l} P_0\dfrac{1}{r} + P_1\dfrac{r'}{r^2} + \ldots\ldots + P_i\dfrac{r'^i}{r^{i+1}} + \ldots \\[2mm] \text{or } P_0\dfrac{1}{r'} + P_1\dfrac{r}{r'^2} + \ldots\ldots + P_i\dfrac{r^i}{r'^{i+1}} + \ldots \end{array}\right\}\ \ \ldots\ldots(1),$$

where $P_0, P_1, \ldots P_i\ldots$ are all determinate rational and entire functions of μ,

$$\sqrt{1-\mu^2}\cos\omega,\ \text{and}\ \sqrt{1-\mu^2}\sin\omega;$$

and the same functions of μ',

$$\sqrt{1-\mu'^2}\cos\omega',\ \text{and}\ \sqrt{1-\mu'^2}\sin\omega'.$$

The general coefficient P_i is of i dimensions in μ,

$$\sqrt{1-\mu^2}\cos\omega,\ \text{and}\ \sqrt{1-\mu^2}\sin\omega.$$

The greatest value of P_i (disregarding its sign) is unity. For if we put

$$\mu\mu' + \sqrt{1-\mu^2}\sqrt{1-\mu'^2}\cos(\omega - \omega') = \cos\phi = \frac{1}{2}\left(\varepsilon + \frac{1}{\varepsilon}\right),$$

2—2

then P_i = coefficient of c^i in

$$(1 + c^2 - 2c \cos \phi)^{-\frac{1}{2}}, \text{ or } (1 - cz)^{-\frac{1}{2}} \left(1 - \frac{c}{z}\right)^{-\frac{1}{2}}$$

= coefficient of c^i in

$$(1 + \frac{1}{2}cz + \frac{1.3}{2.4}c^2 z^2 + \ldots)(1 + \frac{1}{2}\frac{c}{z} + \frac{1.3}{2.4}\frac{c^2}{z^2} + \ldots$$

$$= A\left(z^i + \frac{1}{z^i}\right) + B\left(z^{i-2} + \frac{1}{z^{i-2}}\right) + \ldots$$

$$= 2A \cos i\phi + 2B \cos (i-2)\phi + \ldots$$

$A, B \ldots$ being all positive and finite. The greatest value of this is, when $\phi = 0$. Hence P_i is greatest when $\phi = 0$.

But then P_i = coefficient of c^i in $(1 + c^2 - 2c)^{-\frac{1}{2}}$ or $(1 - c)^{-1}$

= coefficient of c^i in $1 + c + c^2 + \ldots + c^i + \ldots$

= 1.

Hence 1 is the greatest value of P_i. It follows that the first or second of series (1) will be convergent according as r is less than or greater than r'.

To obtain equations for calculating the coefficients P_0, P_1, $\ldots P_i \ldots$ substitute either of the series (1) in the differential equation in R in the last article, and equate the coefficients of the several powers of r to zero. The general term gives the following equation :

$$\frac{d}{d\mu}\left|\left\{(1 - \mu^2)\frac{dP_i}{d\mu}\right\} + \frac{1}{1 - \mu^2}\frac{d^2 P_i}{d\omega^2} + i(i+1)P_i = 0,$$

by integrating which P_i should be determined*. The series for R would then be known.

25. The functions P_0, $P_1 \ldots P_i \ldots$ possess some remarkable properties which were discovered by Laplace. They are therefore called, after him, *Laplace's Coefficients*, of the orders 0, 1, $\ldots i \ldots$ It will be observed that these quantities are definite

---

* For the direct integration of this equation, see two Papers in the *Philosophical Transactions* for 1841 and 1857, by Mr Hargreave and Professor Donkin respectively.

and have no arbitrary constants in them. Laplace's Coefficients are therefore certain definite expressions involving only numerical quantities with μ and ω, μ' and ω'. Any other expressions which may satisfy the partial differential equation in P_i, which is called Laplace's Equation, may be designated *Laplace's Functions* to distinguish them from the " Coefficients." The fundamental properties of these Coefficients and Functions we shall now proceed to demonstrate.

PROP.   *To prove that if Q_i and R_i be two Laplace's Coefficients or Functions, then $\int_{-1}^{1}\int_{0}^{2\pi} Q_i R_{i'} d\mu\, d\omega = 0$, when i and i' are different integers.*

26.   By Laplace's Equation in the last Article

$$i(i+1) Q_i = -\frac{d}{d\mu}\left\{(1-\mu^2)\frac{dQ_i}{d\mu}\right\} - \frac{1}{1-\mu^2}\frac{d^2Q_i}{d\omega^2};$$

$$\therefore \int_{-1}^{1}\int_{0}^{2\pi} Q_i R_{i'}\, d\mu\, d\omega$$

$$= -\frac{1}{i(i+1)}\int_{-1}^{1}\int_{0}^{2\pi}\left[\frac{d}{d\mu}\left\{(1-\mu^2)\frac{dQ_i}{d\mu}\right\} + \frac{1}{1-\mu^2}\frac{d^2Q_i}{d\omega^2}\right] R_{i'}\, d\mu\, d\omega.$$

By a double integration by parts

$$\int \frac{d}{d\mu}\left\{(1-\mu^2)\frac{dQ_i}{d\mu}\right\} R_{i'}\, d\mu = (1-\mu^2)\frac{dQ_i}{d\mu} R_{i'} - (1-\mu^2)\frac{dR_{i'}}{d\mu} Q_i$$

$$+ \int \frac{d}{d\mu}\left\{(1-\mu^2)\frac{dR_{i'}}{d\mu}\right\} Q_i\, d\mu;$$

$$\therefore \int_{-1}^{1}\frac{d}{d\mu}\left\{(1-\mu^2)\frac{dQ_i}{d\mu}\right\} R_{i'}\, d\mu = \int_{-1}^{1}\frac{d}{d\mu}\left\{(1-\mu^2)\frac{dR_{i'}}{d\mu}\right\} Q_i\, d\mu.$$

Again, $\int R_{i'}\frac{d^2Q_i}{d\omega^2}\, d\omega = R_{i'}\frac{dQ_i}{d\omega} - Q_i\frac{dR_{i'}}{d\omega} + \int Q\frac{d^2R_{i'}}{d\omega^2}\, d\omega;$

$$\therefore \int_{0}^{2\pi} R_{i'}\frac{d^2Q_i}{d\omega^2}\, d\omega = \int_{0}^{2\pi} Q_i\frac{d^2R_{i'}}{d\omega^2}\, d\omega,$$

since when $\omega = 0$ and 2π, each of the functions Q_i, $R_{i'}$, $\dfrac{dQ_i}{d\omega}$, $\dfrac{dR_{i'}}{d\omega}$ has the same values, because they are functions of μ,

$$\sqrt{1-\mu^2}\cos\omega \text{ and } \sqrt{1-\mu^2}\sin\omega.$$

Hence, $\displaystyle\int_{-1}^{1}\int_{0}^{2\pi} Q_i R_{i'}\, d\mu\, d\omega$

$$= -\frac{1}{i\,(i+1)}\int_{-1}^{1}\int_{0}^{2\pi}\left[\frac{d}{d\mu}\left\{(1-\mu^2)\frac{dR_{i'}}{d\mu}\right\}+\frac{1}{1-\mu^2}\frac{d^2R_{i'}}{d\omega^2}\right]Q_i\, d\mu\, d\omega$$

$$=\frac{i''(i''+1)}{i\,(i+1)}\int_{-1}^{1}\int_{0}^{2\pi} Q_i R_{i'}\, d\mu\, d\omega,$$

by Laplace's Equation.

Hence, $\displaystyle\int_{-1}^{1}\int_{0}^{2\pi} Q_i\, R_{i'}\, d\mu\, d\omega = 0$, when i and i'' are unequal. When they are the same the equation becomes an identical one, and therefore gives no result.

This property is true also when $i = 0$, as may easily be shown by going through the process of the last Proposition, Q_i being Q_0 or a constant.

PROP. *To prove that a function of μ, $\sqrt{1-\mu^2}\cos\omega$, and $\sqrt{1-\mu^2}\sin\omega$, as $F(\mu, \omega)$, can be expanded in a series of Laplace's Functions; provided that $F(\mu, \omega)$ do not become infinite between the limits -1 and 1 of μ, and 0 and 2π of ω.*

27. This very important Proposition will occupy the present and five following Articles.

Let $\mu\mu' + \sqrt{1-\mu^2}\sqrt{1-\mu'^2}\cos(\omega-\omega') = p$; then by Art. 24,

$$(1+c^2-2cp)^{-\frac{1}{2}} = 1 + P_1 c + P_2 c^2 + \ldots\ldots + P_i c^i + \ldots\ldots$$

c being any quantity not greater than unity.

Differentiate with respect to c,

$$\frac{p-c}{(1+c^2-2cp)^{\frac{3}{2}}} = P_1 + 2P_2 c + \ldots\ldots + iP_i c^{i-1} + \ldots\ldots$$

Multiply this by $2c$ and add it to the former equation.

$$\therefore \frac{1-c^2}{(1+c^2-2cp)^{\frac{3}{2}}} = 1 + 3P_1 c + 5P_2 c^2 + \ldots\ldots + (2i+1)P_i c_i + \ldots$$

Now c being quite arbitrary we may put it $=1$. Then the fraction on the left-hand side of this equation vanishes, except when $p=1$; in which case the fraction on the left hand becomes apparently indeterminate: but it is in reality infinite. For when $p=1$, $\dfrac{1-c^2}{(1+c^2-2cp)^{\frac{3}{2}}} = \dfrac{1+c}{(1-c)^2} = $ infinity, when $c=1$.

When $p=1$, then

$$\cos(\omega'-\omega) = \frac{1-\mu\mu'}{\sqrt{(1-\mu^2)(1-\mu'^2)}} = \sqrt{\frac{1-2\mu\mu'+\mu^2\mu'^2}{1-\mu^2-\mu'^2+\mu^2\mu'^2}},$$

and that this may not be greater than unity we must take $\mu^2+\mu'^2$ not greater than $2\mu\mu'$, or $(\mu-\mu')^2$ not greater than zero. Hence $\mu'=\mu$, and therefore $\cos(\omega'-\omega)=1$, and $\omega'=\omega$.

These, then, are the values of μ' and ω' which make $p=1$.

Hence, the series $1 + 3P_1 + 5P_2 + \ldots\ldots + (2i+1)P_i + \ldots\ldots$ vanishes for all values of μ and ω, μ' and ω', except when $\mu=\mu'$ and $\omega=\omega'$, in which case the sum of its terms suddenly changes from zero to infinity.

28.   Upon this series depends the important property of Laplace's Functions which we are now demonstrating, and which gives them so great a value in the higher branches of analysis. In consequence of the discontinuity above pointed out, and also because the series becomes infinite in one stage of the variations of its variables, it has been considered by some to be unsatisfactory to deduce any properties from it. But the latter objection is entirely removed by the fact, that we do not use the series in its present form, but after being multiplied by small infinitesimal quantities which render the aggregate of its terms finite, preventing their accumulating to an infinite amount. With regard to the objection of discontinuity, there appears to be no sufficient ground for it. There is no question, that the property deduced (as enunciated

in our Proposition) is true, at any rate for rational functions of μ, $\sqrt{1-\mu^2}\cos\omega$, and $\sqrt{1-\mu^2}\sin\omega$, and is also most important. This objection, however, deserves to be examined with care, which we now propose to do in the course of our demonstration.

29. Multiply both sides of the last equation by the double element $d\mu'd\omega'$, and integrate,

$$\int_{-1}^{1}\int_{0}^{2\pi}\frac{(1-c^2)d\mu'd\omega'}{(1+c^2-2cp)^{\frac{3}{2}}}=\int_{-1}^{1}\int_{0}^{2\pi}\{+3cP_1+\ldots+(2i+1)c^iP_i+\ldots\}d\mu'd\omega'.$$

The property of Laplace's Functions proved in Art. 26, shows that every term of the series on the right, except the first, vanishes of itself, independently of the other terms; and therefore (as was before intimated) the terms cannot accumulate. The first term is 4π: and therefore the integral of the fraction on the left, that is

$$\int_{-1}^{1}\int_{0}^{2\pi}\frac{(1-c^2)\,d\mu'd\omega'}{(1+c^2-2cp)^{\frac{3}{2}}},=4\pi.$$

It is remarkable that this result is altogether independent of c.

30. The truth of this may be shown also by integrating the fraction on the left. This cannot readily be done with the co-ordinates as at present chosen. But it may be done by a simple transformation, and a change in the way of taking the elements.

Suppose a sphere of radius unity described about C the origin of co-ordinates. Let θ' and ω' be the angular co-ordinates to a point P, θ' (or $\cos^{-1}\mu'$) measured from a fixed point A along a great circle of the sphere, and ω' the angle which this great circle makes with another and fixed great circle through A. Then $d\theta'.d\omega'\sin\theta'$, or $-d\mu'd\omega'$, is an infinitesimal element of the surface of the sphere at P. Take D a point within the sphere, and let $CD=c$, and sup-

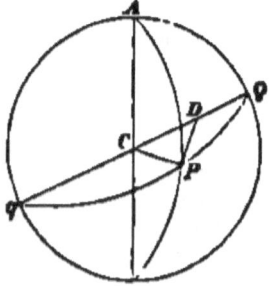

pose CD meets the sphere in Q when produced forwards, and in q when produced backwards. Let μ and ω be the co-ordinates of Q. Then p (see its value, Art. 27) is the cosine of the angle which CP and CQ make with each other: and the distance of P from $D = \sqrt{1 + c^2 - 2cp}$. Let ψ be the angle which the plane CPQ makes with CAQ, that is, the angle AQP. By changing the origin of the angles from A to Q, and dividing the surface of the sphere into new elements, beginning from Q as the origin, the element at P, with these new co-ordinates $\cos^{-1} p$ and ψ, will be $-dp d\psi$.

By reverting to the meaning of integration we see that the integral under consideration $= (1 - c^2) \times$ limit of sum of all the elements of the surface of the sphere divided respectively by the cubes of their distances from D.

But this, by the change of co-ordinates, also

$$= \int_{-1}^{1} \int_{0}^{2\pi} \frac{(1 - c^2)\, dp d\psi}{(1 + c^2 - 2cp)^{\frac{3}{2}}}, \text{ which} = 2\pi (1 - c^2) \int_{-1}^{1} \frac{dp}{(1 + c^2 - 2cp)^{\frac{3}{2}}}$$

$$= 2\pi \frac{1 - c^2}{c} \left(\frac{1}{\sqrt{1 + c^2 - 2cp}} + \text{const.} \right) = 2\pi \frac{1 - c^2}{c} \left(\frac{1}{1 - c} - \frac{1}{1 + c} \right)$$

$= 4\pi$, whatever value c has. This coincides with the former result.

31. This integration helps us to see by what process c disappears from the result; and it will assist us in the latter part of the present demonstration.

The quantity $1 - p$ is the versed-sine of the arc QP, and is measured along the line QCq. Let this line be divided into n parts each equal to h, so that $n \cdot h =$ the diameter $= 2$, n being very large and h very small. Draw perpendiculars to the diameter through these divisions cutting the circle QPq in a series of points; and call the distances of these points from D, beginning from Q,

$$1 - c, \quad s', \quad s'', \quad s''' \ldots \ldots s^{(n-1)}, \quad 1 + c.$$

Suppose P is at the xth division; then

$$1 - p = x \cdot h,$$

and $\qquad d(1 - p) \text{ or } -dp = (x + 1) h - xh = h.$

Then by mere expansion, omitting the squares and higher powers of h as they vanish in the limit with reference to the first power, we see the truth of the following;

$$\frac{'-dp}{(1+c^2-2cp)^{\frac{3}{2}}} = \frac{d(1-p)}{[(1-c)^2+2c(1-p)]^{\frac{3}{2}}}$$

$$= \frac{1}{c}\left\{\frac{1}{\sqrt{(1-c)^2+2cxh}} - \frac{1}{\sqrt{(1-c)^2+2c(x+1)h}}\right\}$$

$$= \frac{1}{c}\left(\frac{1}{s^{(x)}} - \frac{1}{s^{(x+1)}}\right).$$

By giving x its successive values from 0 to $n-1$, and adding together all the resulting values of this expression and taking the limit, we have the integral with respect to p. It matters not in which order we effect the integration. Hence the whole integral

$$= \int_0^{2\pi}\int_{-1}^{1}\frac{(1-c^2)\,d\psi\,dp}{(1+c^2-2cp)^{\frac{3}{2}}}$$

$$= \int_0^{2\pi} d\psi\,\frac{1-c^2}{c}\left\{\left(\frac{1}{1+c}-\frac{1}{s'}\right)+\left(\frac{1}{s'}-\frac{1}{s''}\right)+...+\left(\frac{1}{s^{(n-1)}}-\frac{1}{1+c}\right)\right\},$$

n being made infinitely great,

$$= \int_0^{2\pi} d\psi\,\frac{1-c^2}{c}\left\{\frac{1}{1-c}-\frac{1}{1+c}+\left(\frac{1}{s'}-\frac{1}{s'}\right)+...+\left(\frac{1}{s^{(n-1)}}-\frac{1}{s^{(n-1)}}\right)\right\}$$

$$= \int_0^{2\pi} d\psi\left[2+\frac{1-c^2}{c}\left\{\left(\frac{1}{s'}-\frac{1}{s'}\right)+...+\left(\frac{1}{s^{(n-1)}}-\frac{1}{s^{(n-1)}}\right)\right\}\right].$$

Here it will be seen that the terms within the last brackets mutually destroy each other whatever be the value of c. It may also be observed that were this not the case, that whole part of the expression would vanish for the particular value $c=1$ (which is the only case we shall have to use), whatever the value of the sum of the terms following the multiplier $1-c^2$, so long as that sum is not infinite.

32. Suppose now $F(\mu', \omega')$ is any function of μ' and ω', then

$$\int_{-1}^{1}\int_{0}^{2\pi} (1 - c^2)\, \frac{F(\mu', \omega')\, d\mu' d\omega'}{(1 + c^2 - 2cp)^{\frac{3}{2}}}$$

$$= \int_{-1}^{1}\int_{0}^{2\pi} \{1 + 3P_1 + \dots + (2i + 1) P_i + \dots\}\, F(\mu', \omega')\, d\mu' d\omega'.$$

The reasoning above enables us now to prove that the integral on the left-hand side $= 4\pi F(\mu, \omega)$, which directly leads to the theorem we are wishing to demonstrate.

The function $F(\mu', \omega')$ at the point Q is $F(\mu, \omega)$, call it F: let $F', F''\dots F^{(n)}$ be its values at the points of junction of the successive elements along the great circle QPq. Then by multiplying the successive values of $\frac{1}{c}\left(\frac{1}{s^{(n)}} - \frac{1}{s^{(n+1)}}\right)$ by $F, F', F''\dots$ and adding them together, we have

$$\int_{-1}^{1}\int_{0}^{2\pi} (1 - c^2)\, \frac{F(\mu', \omega')\, d\mu' d\omega'}{(1 + c^2 - 2cp)^{\frac{3}{2}}},$$

or $$\int_{0}^{2\pi}\int_{-1}^{1} (1 - c^2)\, \frac{F(\mu', \omega')\, d\psi\, dp}{(1 + c^2 - 2cp)^{\frac{3}{2}}},$$

$$= \int_{0}^{2\pi} d\psi\, \frac{1 - c^2}{c}\left\{\left(\frac{1}{1-c} - \frac{1}{s}\right)F + \left(\frac{1}{s} - \frac{1}{s'}\right)F' + \dots + \left(\frac{1}{s^{(n-1)}} - \frac{1}{1+c}\right)F^{(n-1)}\right\}$$

$$= \int_{0}^{2\pi} d\psi\left[\frac{1+c}{c}F - \frac{1-c}{c}F^{(n-1)} + \frac{1-c^2}{c}\left\{\left(\frac{F'}{s} - \frac{F}{s}\right) + \left(\frac{F''}{s'} - \frac{F'}{s'}\right) + \dots\right\}\right]$$

$$= \int_{0}^{2\pi} d\psi\left[\frac{1+c}{c}F - \frac{1-c}{c}F^{(n-1)} + \frac{1+c}{c}\left\{(F'-F)\frac{1-c}{s} + (F''-F')\frac{1-c}{s'} + \dots\right\}\right],$$

n being made infinitely great.

The fractions $\frac{1-c}{s'}, \frac{1-c}{s''}, \dots$ diminish successively in value, being the ratios of QD to the successive values of DP. When $c = 1$ each of them vanishes; and in the limit none of the factors $F' - F, F'' - F', \dots$ become infinite. Hence the integral $= \int_{0}^{2\pi} d\psi . 2F$, when $c = 1$, $= 4\pi F(\mu, \omega)$ because $F(\mu, \omega)$

is a function of μ and ω only, and is altogether independent of ψ.

$$\therefore\ 4\pi F(\mu,\omega)=\int_{-1}^{1}\int_{0}^{2\pi}[1+3P_1+\dots+(2i+1)P_i+\dots]F(\mu',\omega')d\mu'd\omega';$$

$$\therefore\ F(\mu,\omega)=\int_{-1}^{1}\int_{0}^{2\pi}\left\{\frac{F(\mu',\omega')}{4\pi}+\frac{3F(\mu',\omega')}{4\pi}P_1+\dots\dots\right.$$
$$\left.+\frac{(2i+1)F(\mu',\omega')}{4\pi}P_i+\dots\dots\right\}d\mu'd\omega'.$$

The general term of this, viz.

$$\int_{-1}^{1}\int_{0}^{2\pi}\frac{2i+1}{4\pi}F(\mu',\omega')P_id\mu'd\omega',$$

which we will call F_i, is a function of μ and ω; and evidently satisfies Laplace's Equation in μ and ω, because P_i does so. Hence, this is a Laplace's Function, of the ith order: and the result is, what we were to demonstrate, that any function of μ and ω may be expanded in a series of Laplace's Functions; or,

$$F(\mu,\omega)=F_0+F_1+F_2+\dots\dots+F_i+\dots\dots$$

33. Those who are at all acquainted with the controversy which followed the first discovery of these remarkable functions by Laplace, will understand why we have entered so fully upon the subject. Laplace's demonstration in the *Mécanique Céleste* was by no means conclusive. This Mr Ivory pointed out in the *Philosophical Transactions* for 1812; and in the Volume for 1822 he threw considerable doubt upon the applicability of the theorem to functions that are not rational and entire functions of μ, $\sqrt{1-\mu^2}\cos\omega$, $\sqrt{1-\mu^2}\sin\omega$. Poisson has written much upon the subject. In the first edition of the author's *Mechanical Philosophy* the last method of Poisson was followed, as given in his *Théorie Mathématique de la Chaleur;* in which he effects the integration of the fraction on the left-hand side by the artifice of substituting for it an integrable, but entirely different fraction in its general form, but which coincides with it in the particular case for which he requires it in the result, viz. when $c=1$. In the Second

Edition of the *Mechanical Philosophy* we gave a much shorter proof, based upon an idea taken from Professor O'Brien's *Mathematical Tracts*. But this also rather concealed the real difficulty of the case, and passed it over by an artifice. In the demonstration now given, we have gone to the foundation of the calculus, the doctrine of limits, and attempted to clear up all difficulty and ambiguity in the matter.

With regard to the doubt thrown out by Ivory, alluded to above, it seems to be clear that theoretically every function can be expanded in a series of Laplace's Functions: but if it be not a rational function of the co-ordinates, the number of terms in the series will be infinite, and if the terms be not convergent, the expansion, or rather arrangement, will be useless. But this must be determined in each case. A similar uncertainty, requiring examination, always attends the use of infinite series.

PROP. *To prove that a function of μ and ω can be arranged in only one series of Laplace's Functions.*

34.   For if possible let both these be true,

$$F(\mu, \omega) = F_0 + F_1 + F_2 + \ldots\ldots + F_i + \ldots\ldots$$

$$F(\mu, \omega) = G_0 + G_1 + G_2 + \ldots\ldots + G + \ldots\ldots$$

$$\therefore 0 = (F_0 - G_0) + (F_1 - G_1) + \ldots\ldots + (F_i - G_i) + \ldots\ldots$$

and if these letters be accented when μ' and ω' are the variables instead of μ and ω, then

$$0 = (F_0' - G_0') + (F_1' - G_1') + \ldots\ldots + (F_i' - G_i') + \ldots\ldots$$

$$\therefore 0 = \int_{-1}^{1}\int_{0}^{2\pi} P_i (F_i' - G_i')\, d\mu'\, d\omega', \text{ by Art. 26.}$$

But the principle demonstrated in the last Proposition shows that

$$F_i - G_i = \frac{1}{4\pi}\int_{-1}^{1}\int_{0}^{2\pi}(1 + 3P_1 + \ldots)\,(F_i' - G_i')\, d\mu'\, d\omega',$$

$$= \frac{2i+1}{4\pi}\int_{-1}^{1}\int_{0}^{2\pi} P_i (F_i' - G_i')\, d\mu'\, d\omega', \text{ by Art. 26,}$$

$$= 0, \text{ by the condition deduced above;}$$

therefore $F_i = G_i$, and the two series are term by term identical, and the Proposition is true.

35. It follows from this, that if by any process we can expand a function in a series of quantities which satisfy Laplace's Equation, that is the only series of the kind into which it can be expanded: and if by any other process we obtain what is apparently another, the terms of the two series must be the same, term by term, and we may put them equal to each other.

36. Before concluding this Chapter, we shall explain how the numerical coefficients in $P_0 P_1 \ldots P_i \ldots$ are found: and shall give a few examples of the truth of the last Proposition but one (that in Art. 32) by actual integration.

PROP. *To explain how to expand P_i.*

37. By Art. 24 P_i is the coefficient of c^i in the expansion of the function

$$[1 + c^2 - 2c \left[\mu\mu' + \sqrt{1-\mu^2}\sqrt{1-\mu'^2}\cos(\omega-\omega')\right]]^{-\frac{1}{2}},$$

and is therefore a rational and entire function of μ,

$$\sqrt{1-\mu^2}\cos\omega, \text{ and } \sqrt{1-\mu^2}\sin\omega;$$

and is precisely the same function of μ',

$$\sqrt{1-\mu'^2}\cos\omega', \text{ and } \sqrt{1-\mu'^2}\sin\omega'.$$

The general term of P_i, viz. that involving $\cos n(\omega-\omega')$, can arise solely from the powers n, $n+2$, $n+4$, ... of $\cos(\omega-\omega')$. Hence $(1-\mu^2)^{\frac{n}{2}}$ will occur as a factor of that term: and the other part of its coefficient will be a factor of the form

$$A_0\mu^{i-n} + A_1\mu^{i-n-1} + \ldots + A_r\mu^{i-n-2r} + \ldots = H_n \text{ suppose.}$$

Hence

$$P_i = H_0 + (1-\mu^2)^1 H_1\cos(\omega-\omega') + \ldots + (1-\mu^2)^{\frac{n}{2}} H_n\cos n(\omega-\omega') + \ldots$$

If this be substituted for P_i in Laplace's Equation and the coefficient of $\cos n(\omega-\omega')$ be equated to zero, we obtain a condition from which to calculate the arbitrary constants we have introduced. This condition, after reduction and arrangement, is as follows:

$$0 = (i - n)(i + n + 1) H_s (1 - \mu^2)^s + \frac{d}{d\mu} \left\{ (1 - \mu^2)^{s+1} \frac{dH_s}{d\mu} \right\}.$$

Substituting in this the series which H_s represents, and equating the coefficient of the general term $(1 - \mu^2)^s \mu^{i-s-2}$ to zero, and reducing, we arrive at the formula

$$A_s = - \frac{(i - n - 2s + 2)(i - n - 2s + 1)}{2s(2i - 2s + 1)} A_{s-1}.$$

By making s successively equal 1, 2, 3 ... we have $A_1 A_2 ...$ in terms of A_0. Let these be substituted, and we have the coefficient of $\cos n (\omega - \omega') =$

$$A_0 (1 - \mu^2)^{\frac{i}{2}} \left\{ \mu^{i-n} - \frac{(i - n)(i - n - 1)}{2(2i - 1)} \mu^{i-n-2} + ... \right\},$$

call this $A_0 f(\mu)$. The coefficient A_0 is a function of μ', but is independent of μ: and because P_i is the same function of μ' that it is of μ, it follows that $A_0 = a_n f(\mu')$, where a_n is a numerical quantity: and the coefficient of

$$\cos n (\omega - \omega') = a_n f(\mu') f(\mu).$$

To find a_n we must compare the first term of the ascending expansion of $a_n f(\mu') f(\mu)$ in powers of μ with the corresponding term in the coefficient of c^i in the actual expansion of

$$[1 + c^2 - 2c [\mu\mu' + \sqrt{1 - \mu^2} \sqrt{1 - \mu'^2} \cos (\omega - \omega')]]^{-1}.$$

This leads to the following result:

$$a_n = 2 \left\{ \frac{1 . 3 . 5 ... (2i - 1)}{1 . 2 . 3 ... i} \right\}^2 \frac{i (i - 1) ... (i - n + 1)}{(i + 1)(i + 2) ... (i + n)};$$

this applies when $n = 1, 2, 3 ...$, but evidently not when $n = 0$: a_0 is found by equating coefficients to be

$$\left\{ \frac{1 . 2 . 3 ... (2i - 1)}{1 . 2 . 3 ... i} \right\}^2.$$

We have now the complete value of P_i in a series; it is as follows:

$$P_i = \left\{ \frac{1 \cdot 3 \cdot 5 \ldots (2i-1)}{1 \cdot 2 \cdot 3 \ldots i} \right\}^2$$

$$\times \left[\left\{ \mu^i - \frac{i(i-1)}{2(2i-1)} \mu^{i-2} + \frac{i(i-1)}{2(2i-1)} \frac{(i-2)(i-3)}{4(2i-3)} \mu^{i-4} - \&c \ldots \right\} \right.$$

$$\times \left\{ \mu'^i - \frac{i(i-1)}{2(2i-1)} \mu'^{i-2} + \frac{i(i-1)}{2(2i-1)} \frac{(i-2)(i-3)}{4(2i-3)} \mu'^{i-4} - \&c \ldots \right\}$$

$$+ 2 \cos(\omega - \omega') \frac{i}{i+1}$$

$$\times (1-\mu^2)^{\frac{1}{2}} \left\{ \mu^{i-1} - \frac{(i-1)(i-2)}{2(2i-1)} \mu^{i-3} + \frac{(i-1)(i-2)}{2(2i-1)} \frac{(i-3)(i-4)}{4(2i-3)} \mu^{i-5} \ldots \right\}$$

$$\times (1-\mu'^2)^{\frac{1}{2}} \left\{ \mu'^{i-1} - \frac{(i-1)(i-2)}{2(2i-1)} \mu'^{i-3} + \frac{(i-1)(i-2)}{2(2i-1)} \frac{(i-3)(i-4)}{4(2i-3)} \mu'^{i-5} \ldots \right\}$$

$$+ 2 \cos 2(\omega - \omega') \frac{i(i-1)}{(i+1)(i+2)}$$

$$\times (1-\mu^2) \left\{ \mu^{i-2} - \frac{(i-2)(i-3)}{2(2i-1)} \mu^{i-4} + \frac{(i-2)(i-3)}{2(2i-1)} \frac{(i-4)(i-5)}{4(2i-3)} \mu^{i-6} \ldots \right\}$$

$$\times (1-\mu'^2) \left\{ \mu'^{i-2} - \frac{(i-2)(i-3)}{2(2i-1)} \mu'^{i-4} + \frac{(i-2)(i-3)}{2(2i-1)} \frac{(i-4)(i-3)}{4(2i-3)} \mu'^{i-6} \ldots \right\}$$

$$+ \&c \ldots \right].$$

38. The following numerical examples are written down for convenience of reference:

(1) $P_1 = \mu\mu' + \sqrt{1-\mu^2} \sqrt{1-\mu'^2} \cos(\omega - \omega')$.

(2) $P_2 = \frac{9}{4} \left\{ \left(\mu^2 - \frac{1}{3} \right) \left(\mu'^2 - \frac{1}{3} \right) + \frac{4}{3} (1-\mu^2)^{\frac{1}{2}} \mu (1-\mu'^2)^{\frac{1}{2}} \mu' \cos(\omega - \omega') \right.$

$$\left. + \frac{1}{3} (1-\mu^2)(1-\mu'^2) \cos 2(\omega - \omega') \right\}.$$

(3) $\quad P_9 = \dfrac{25}{4}\left\{\left(\mu^2 - \dfrac{3}{5}\mu\right)\left(\mu'^2 - \dfrac{3}{5}\mu'\right)\right.$

$\qquad + \dfrac{3}{2}(1-\mu^2)^{\frac12}\left(\mu^2 - \dfrac{1}{5}\right)(1-\mu'^2)^{\frac12}\left(\mu'^2 - \dfrac{1}{5}\right)\cos(\omega - \omega')$

$+\dfrac{3}{5}(1-\mu^2)\mu(1-\mu'^2)\mu'\cos 2(\omega - \omega') + \dfrac{1}{10}(1-\mu^2)^{\frac32}(1-\mu'^2)^{\frac32}\cos 3(\omega - \omega')\left.\right\}$

&c. = &c.

39. The following are some examples of expanding a function in a series of Laplace's Functions, by an application of the formula

$$F_i = \frac{2i+1}{4\pi}\int_{-1}^{1}\int_{0}^{2\pi} F(\mu', \omega')\, P_i d\mu' d\omega',$$

proved in Art. 32.

Ex. 1. Arrange $a + b\mu^2$ in terms of Laplace's Functions.

Here $F(\mu', \omega') = a + b\mu'^2$. First put $i = 0$, $P_0 = 1$;

$$\therefore F_0 = \frac{1}{4\pi}\int_{-1}^{1}\int_{0}^{2\pi}(a + b\mu'^2)\,d\mu' d\omega' = \frac{1}{2}\int_{-1}^{1}(a + b\mu'^2)\,d\mu'$$

$$= \frac{1}{2}\left(a\mu' + \frac{1}{3}b\mu'^3 + \text{const.}\right) = a + \frac{1}{3}b.$$

Again, put $i = 1$, P_1 is found in the last Article.

$$\therefore F_1 = \frac{3}{4\pi}\int_{-1}^{1}\int_{0}^{2\pi}(a+b\mu'^2)[\mu\mu' + \sqrt{1-\mu^2}\sqrt{1-\mu'^2}\cos(\omega-\omega')]d\mu' d\omega'$$

$$= \frac{3}{4\pi}\int_{-1}^{1}(a+b\mu'^2)\,[\mu\mu'.\,\omega' - \sqrt{1-\mu^2}\sqrt{1-\mu'^2}\sin(\omega-\omega')]\,d\mu',$$

between the proper limits, $\omega' = 0$ and $\omega' = 2\pi$,

$$= \frac{3}{2}\int_{-1}^{1}(a+b\mu'^2)\,\mu\mu' d\mu' = \frac{3}{2}\mu\left(\frac{1}{2}a\mu'^2 + \frac{1}{4}b\mu'^4\right),$$

between the limits $\mu' = -1$ and $\mu' = 1$, $= 0$.

P. A.   3

Next, put $i = 2$, and substitute for P_2 from the last Article.

$$\therefore F_2 = \frac{5}{4\pi} \int_{-1}^{1} \int_{0}^{2\pi} (a + b\mu'^2) \left\{ \frac{9}{4} \left(\mu^2 - \frac{1}{3} \right) \left(\mu'^2 - \frac{1}{3} \right) + M \cos(\omega - \omega') \right.$$

$$\left. + N \cos 2 (\omega - \omega') \right\} d\mu' d\omega'$$

$$= \frac{5}{2} \int_{-1}^{1} (a + b\mu'^2) \frac{9}{4} \left(\mu^2 - \frac{1}{3} \right) \left(\mu'^2 - \frac{1}{3} \right) d\mu'$$

$$= \frac{45}{8} \left(\mu^2 - \frac{1}{3} \right) \int_{-1}^{1} \left\{ -\frac{1}{3} a + \left(a - \frac{1}{3} b \right) \mu'^2 + b\mu'^4 \right\} d\mu'$$

$$= \frac{45}{8} \left(\mu^2 - \frac{1}{3} \right) \left\{ -\frac{2}{3} a + \frac{2}{3} \left(a - \frac{1}{3} b \right) + \frac{2}{5} b \right\} = b \left(\mu^2 - \frac{1}{3} \right).$$

Hence the function $a + b\mu^2$ stands as follows, when arranged in terms of Laplace's Functions,

$$\left(a + \frac{1}{3} b \right) + b \left(\mu^2 - \frac{1}{3} \right),$$

and consists of two Functions, of the order 0 and 2 respectively. The above is a long process to arrive at this result. It might have been so arranged at a glance. But the calculation has been given as an example of the use of the formula, which in most cases is the only means of obtaining the desired result.

Ex. 2.   Arrange $49 + 30\mu + 3\mu^2 + \sqrt{1 - \mu^2}\,(40 + 72\mu) \cos(\omega - \alpha)$

$+ 24 (1 - \mu^2) \cos 2 (\omega - \alpha)$ in terms of Laplace's Functions.

The result is $50 + \{30\mu + 40 \sqrt{1 - \mu^2} \cos(\omega - \alpha)\}$

$+ \{3\mu^2 - 1 + 72\mu \sqrt{1 - \mu^2} \cos(\omega - \alpha) + 24 (1 - \mu^2) \cos 2 (\omega - \alpha)\},$

consisting of three functions of the orders 0, 1, 2.

Ex. 3.   Let the function be

$$1 + \sqrt{2 - 2\mu^2} \cos(\omega + \alpha) + \frac{1}{2} (1 - \mu^2) \cos 2 (\omega + \alpha).$$

The first term is a Laplace's Function of the order 0, and the second and third terms taken together are one of the second order.

Ex. 4. Let $1-(1-\mu^2)\cos^2\omega$ be the function. The arrangement is

$$\frac{2}{3}+\frac{1}{2}\left\{\left(\mu^2-\frac{1}{3}\right)-(1-\mu^2)\cos 2\omega\right\},$$

or, which is the same,

$$\frac{2}{3}+\left\{\frac{1}{3}-(1-\mu^2)\cos^2\omega\right\}.$$

CHAPTER III.

ATTRACTION OF BODIES NEARLY SPHERICAL.

40. As the Earth and other bodies of the Solar System are nearly spherical, and yet may not be precisely of the spheroidal form, it is found necessary in questions of Physical Astronomy to calculate the attraction of bodies nearly spherical. It is in these calculations that the value of the Functions we have been considering in the last Chapter is seen.

If $r'\theta'\omega'$ be the co-ordinates to any element of the attracting mass, ρ' be its density, and $\cos\theta' = \mu'$, then the mass of this element

$$= \rho'dr'\,r'd\theta'\,r'\sin\theta'd\omega' = -\rho'r''^2dr'd\mu'd\omega',$$

and the reciprocal of the distance being R, by Art. 18 and 24, the potential V

$$= \int_0^r\int_{-1}^1\int_0^{2\pi} \rho'\left(P_0\frac{r''}{r} + P_1\frac{r''^2}{r^2} + \dots + P_i\frac{r''^{i+1}}{r^{i+1}} + \dots\right)dr'd\mu'd\omega';$$

or $$\int_0^r\int_{-1}^1\int_0^{2\pi} \rho'\left(P_0r' + P_1r + P_2\frac{r^2}{r'} + \dots + P_i\frac{r^i}{r'^{i-1}} + \dots\right)dr'd\mu'd\omega',$$

according as r, the distance of the attracted point from the origin, is greater or less than r'. We shall proceed soon to use these formulæ; but we must first find the value of V for a perfect sphere.

PROP. *To calculate the value of V for a homogeneous sphere.*

41. Let the centre of the sphere be the origin of the polar co-ordinates $(r'\mu'\omega')$ to any element of its mass, and the line through the attracted point be that from which the angles are

measured, and ρ the density. Then $-\rho r'^2 dr' d\mu' d\omega'$ is the mass of the element: its distance from the attracted point

$$= \sqrt{r^2 + r'^2 - 2rr' \cos \omega}.$$

Hence, a being the radius of the sphere,

$$V = \int_0^a \int_{-1}^1 \int_0^{2\pi} \frac{\rho r'^2 dr' d\mu' d\omega'}{\sqrt{r^2 + r'^2 - 2rr'\mu'}}$$

$$= 2\pi\rho \int_0^a \int_{-1}^1 \frac{r'^2 dr' d\mu'}{\sqrt{r^2 + r'^2 - 2rr'\mu'}} = 2\pi\rho \int_0^a -\frac{r'}{r}\left\{\sqrt{r^2 + r'^2 - 2rr'\mu'}\right\} dr',$$

from $\mu' = -1$ to $\mu' = 1$, $= 2\pi\rho \int_0^a \frac{r'}{r}\left\{(r+r') \mp (r-r')\right\} dr'$,

— when the attracted point is without, and + when it is within the shell,

$$= \frac{4\pi\rho}{r} \int_0^a r'^2 dr' = \frac{4\pi\rho a^3}{3r},$$

when the point is without the sphere.

When the point is within the sphere, the part of V for the shells which enclose the point

$$= 2\pi\rho \int_r^a 2r' dr' = 2\pi\rho (a^2 - r^2):$$

and the part of V for the other shells of the sphere

$$= \frac{4\pi\rho}{r} \int_0^r r'^2 dr' = \frac{4}{3}\pi\rho r^2.$$

Hence $V = \dfrac{4\pi\rho a^3}{3r}$ for an *external* particle,

$$V = 2\pi\rho a^2 - \frac{2}{3}\pi\rho r^2 \text{ for an internal particle.}$$

PROP. *To find the attraction of a homogeneous body, differ-ing little from a sphere in form, on a particle without it.*

42. Since the attracted particle is without the attracting mass, we must expand V in a descending series of powers of r, and shall therefore use the first of the expressions for V in Art. 40. Let the mean radius of the body $= a$; and let $a(1+y')$ be the variable radius, y' being a function of μ' and ω', and its square being neglected.

Then, for the excess of the attracting mass over the sphere of which the radius $= a$, effecting the integration with respect to r' from $r' = a$ to $r' = a(1+y')$, the value of V

$$= \rho \int_{-1}^{1} \int_{0}^{2\pi} \left\{ \frac{a^3}{r} P_0 + \frac{a^4}{r^2} P_1 + \ldots + \frac{a^{i+3}}{r^{i+1}} P_i + \ldots \right\} y' d\mu' d\omega'.$$

But if y, the same function of μ and ω that y' is of μ' and ω', be expanded in a series of Laplace's Functions, viz.

$$Y_0 + Y_1 + \ldots + Y_i + \ldots,$$

then the theorems of Art. 26 and 32 show that

$$\frac{2i+1}{4\pi} \int_{-1}^{1} \int_{0}^{2\pi} y' P_i d\mu' d\omega' = \frac{2i+1}{4\pi} \int_{-1}^{1} \int_{0}^{2\pi} Y_i' P_i d\mu' d\omega' = Y_i.$$

Hence the value of V for the excess over the sphere becomes

$$= \frac{4\pi\rho a^3}{r} \left\{ Y_0 + \frac{a}{3r} Y_1 + \ldots + \frac{a^i}{(2i+1)r^i} Y_i + \ldots \right\};$$

and the part of V for the sphere, rad. $= a$, is

$$V = \frac{4\pi\rho a^3}{3r}.$$

Hence for the whole mass

$$V = \frac{4\pi\rho a^3}{3r} + \frac{4\pi\rho a^3}{r} \left\{ Y_0 + \frac{a}{3r} Y_1 + \ldots + \frac{a^i}{(2i+1)r^i} Y_i + \ldots \right\}.$$

This is the first example in which we see the great value of the properties of Laplace's Functions; they here give us at once the integrals involved in our expression for V, in terms of the equation to the surface of the attracting mass, without integration.

From the expression for V the attraction can be immediately found by the formula of Art. 20. Thus

$$\text{attraction} = -\frac{dV}{dr}$$

$$= \frac{4\pi\rho a^3}{3r^2} + \frac{4\pi\rho a^2}{r^2}\left\{Y_0 + \frac{2a}{3r}\,Y_1 + \dots \frac{(i+1)a^i}{(2i+1)r^i}\,Y_i + \dots\right\}.$$

PROP. *To find the attraction of a homogeneous body, differing but little from a sphere, on a particle within its mass.*

43. We must in this case expand V in an ascending series of powers of r; and shall therefore take the second of the series of Art. 40. By proceeding as in the last Proposition, we find that the part of V which appertains to the excess over the sphere

$$= \rho \int_{-1}^{1}\int_{0}^{2\pi}\left\{a^2 P_0 + ar P_1 + \dots + \frac{r^i}{a^{i-2}}\,P_i + \dots\right\}y'\,d\mu'\,d\omega',$$

or $$= 4\pi\rho a^2\left\{Y_0 + \frac{r}{3a}\,Y_1 + \dots + \frac{r^i}{(2i+1)a^i}\,Y_i + \dots\right\}.$$

Adding to this the part of V which appertains to the sphere of radius a, viz. $2\pi\rho a^2 - \frac{2}{3}\pi\rho r^2$, for the whole mass,

$$V = 2\pi\rho a^2 - \frac{2}{3}\pi\rho r^2 + 4\pi\rho a^2\left\{Y_0 + \frac{r}{3a}\,Y_1 + \dots + \frac{r^i}{(2i+1)a^i}\,Y_i + \dots\right\}.$$

And the attraction $= -\dfrac{dV}{dr}$

$$= \frac{4\pi}{3}\rho r - 4\pi\rho a\left\{\frac{1}{3}\,Y_1 + \frac{2r}{5a}\,Y_2 + \dots + \frac{ir^{i-1}}{(2i+1)a^{i-1}}\,Y_i + \dots\right\}.$$

We can show that by properly choosing the value of (a) and the origin of the radius of the surface we can make Y_0 and Y_1 disappear from the above formulæ.

Prop. *To show that by choosing* a *equal to the radius of the sphere of which the mass equals that of the attracting body we cause Y_0 to vanish, and by taking the centre of gravity of the body as the origin of the radius vector, we cause Y_1 to vanish.*

44.   The mass of the body

$$= \rho \int_0^r \int_{-1}^1 \int_0^{2\pi} r^2 \, dr \, d\mu \, d\omega = \frac{1}{3} \rho \int_{-1}^1 \int_0^{2\pi} r^3 \, d\mu \, d\omega,$$

where r is the radius vector of the surface of the body, and $= a(1+y)$ suppose.   Putting this for r mass of body

$$= \text{mass of sphere (rad.} = a) + \rho a^3 \int_{-1}^1 \int_0^{2\pi} y \, d\mu \, d\omega$$

$$= \text{mass of sphere} + \rho a^3 \int_{-1}^1 \int_0^{2\pi} Y_0, \text{ by Art. 26,}$$

$$= \text{mass of sphere} + 4\pi \rho a^3 Y_0.$$

If then a be taken equal to the radius of the sphere of which the mass equals the mass of the body, $Y_0 = 0$, as was stated.

Again, let $\bar{x} \, \bar{y} \, \bar{z}$ be the co-ordinates to the centre of gravity of the body, M its mass: the co-ordinates to the element of which the mass is $-\rho r^2 \, dr \, d\mu \, d\omega$ are

$$r \sqrt{1-\mu^2} \cos \omega, \quad r \sqrt{1-\mu^2} \sin \omega, \quad \text{and } r\mu;$$

$$\therefore M \cdot \bar{x} = \int_0^r \int_{-1}^1 \int_0^{2\pi} \rho r^3 \sqrt{1-\mu^2} \cos \omega \, dr \, d\mu \, d\omega$$

$$= \frac{1}{4} \int_{-1}^1 \int_0^{2\pi} \rho r^4 \sqrt{1-\mu^2} \cos \omega \, d\mu \, d\omega,$$

$$M \cdot \bar{y} = \int_0^r \int_{-1}^1 \int_0^{2\pi} \rho r^3 \sqrt{1-\mu^2} \sin \omega \, dr \, d\mu \, d\omega$$

$$= \frac{1}{4} \int_{-1}^1 \int_0^{2\pi} \rho r^4 \sqrt{1-\mu^2} \sin \omega \, d\mu \, d\omega,$$

$$M \cdot \bar{z} = \int_0^r \int_{-1}^1 \int_0^{2\pi} \rho r^3 \mu \, dr \, d\mu \, d\omega = \frac{1}{4} \int_{-1}^1 \int_0^{2\pi} r^4 \mu \, d\mu \, d\omega;$$

putting $r = a(1 + y) = a(1 + Y_0 + Y_1 + \ldots + Y_i + \ldots)$, and observing that $\sqrt{1 - \mu^2} \cos \omega$, $\sqrt{1 - \mu^2} \sin \omega$, and μ satisfy Laplace's Equation, and are of the first order, we have by Art. 26,

$$M \cdot \bar{x} = \rho a^4 \int_{-1}^1 \int_0^{2\pi} Y_1 \sqrt{1 - \mu^2} \cos \omega \, d\mu \, d\omega,$$

$$M \cdot \bar{y} = \rho a^4 \int_{-1}^1 \int_0^{2\pi} Y_1 \sqrt{1 - \mu^2} \sin \omega \, d\mu \, d\omega,$$

$$M \cdot \bar{z} = \rho a^4 \int_{-1}^1 \int_0^{2\pi} Y_1 \mu \, d\mu \, d\omega.$$

But Y_1, being a function of μ, $\sqrt{1 - \mu^2} \cos \omega$, and $\sqrt{1 - \mu^2} \sin \omega$ of the first order, is of the form

$$A \sqrt{1 - \mu^2} \cos \omega + B \sqrt{1 - \mu^2} \sin \omega + C\mu;$$

$$\therefore \ M \cdot \bar{x} = \frac{4}{3} \pi \rho a^4 A, \quad M \cdot \bar{y} = \frac{4}{3} \pi \rho a^4 B, \quad M \cdot \bar{z} = \frac{4}{3} \pi \rho a^4 C.$$

Hence if we take the origin of co-ordinates at the centre of gravity and therefore $\bar{x} = 0$, $\bar{y} = 0$, $\bar{z} = 0$, we have $A = 0$, $B = 0$, $C = 0$, and therefore $Y_1 = 0$, as stated in the enunciation.

PROP. *To find the attraction of a heterogeneous body upon a particle without it; the body consisting of thin strata nearly spherical, homogeneous in themselves, but differing one from another in density.*

45. Let $a'(1 + y')$ be the radius of the external surface of any stratum, a' being chosen so that

$$y' = Y_1' + Y_2' + \ldots + Y_i' + \ldots \text{ (Art. 44).}$$

Since the strata are supposed not to be similar to one another, y' is a function of a' as well as of μ' and ω'. Let ρ' be the density of the stratum of which the mean radius is a'. Now the value of V for this stratum equals the difference between the values of V for two homogeneous bodies of the density ρ' and mean radii a' and $a'-da'$. But for the body of which the mean radius is a' (Art. 42)

$$V = \frac{4\pi\rho'a'^{3}}{3r} + \frac{4\pi\rho'a'^{3}}{r}\left\{\frac{a'}{3r}\,Y_{1}' + \dots + \frac{a'^{i}}{(2i+1)\,r^{i}}\,Y_{i}' + \dots\right\}.$$

Hence for the stratum of which the external mean radius is a',

$$V = \frac{4\pi\rho'a'^{3}}{r}\,da' + \frac{4\pi\rho'}{r}\frac{d}{da'}\left\{\frac{a'^{4}}{3r}\,Y_{1}' + \dots + \frac{a'^{i+3}}{(2i+1)r^{i}}\,Y_{i}' + \dots\right\}da',$$

and therefore for the whole body,

$$V = \frac{4\pi}{r}\int_{0}^{a}\rho'\left\{a'^{2} + \frac{d}{da'}\left(\frac{a'^{4}}{3r}\,Y_{1}' + \dots + \frac{a'^{i+3}}{(2i+1)\,r^{i}}\,Y_{i}' + \dots\right)\right\}da'.$$

From which the attraction is easily deduced.

PROP. *To find the attraction of the same body on an internal particle.*

46. Let $r = a(1+y)$ be the radius of the stratum in which the attracted particle lies. Then for the strata within the surface of which the radius is $a(1+y)$, we have

$$V = \frac{4\pi}{r}\int_{0}^{a}\rho'\left\{a'^{2} + \frac{d}{da'}\left(\frac{a'^{4}}{3r}\,Y_{1}' + \dots + \frac{a'^{i+3}}{(2i+1)\,r^{i}}\,Y_{i}' + \dots\right)\right\}da'.$$

But for a stratum external to the particle we have by Art. 43,

$$V = 4\pi\rho'a'da' + 4\pi\rho'\frac{d}{da'}\left\{\frac{ra'}{3}\,Y_{1}' + \dots + \frac{r^{i}}{(2i+1)\,a'^{i-1}}\,Y_{i}' + \dots\right\}da',$$

Consequently for the whole body,

$$V = \frac{4\pi}{r}\int_{0}^{a}\rho'\left\{a'^{2} + \frac{d}{da'}\left(\frac{a'^{4}}{3r}\,Y_{1}' + \dots + \frac{a'^{i+3}}{(2i+1)\,r^{i}}\,Y_{i}' + \dots\right)\right\}da'$$

$$+ 4\pi\int_{a}^{a}\rho'\left\{a'da' + \frac{d}{da'}\left(\frac{ra'}{3}\,Y_{1}' + \dots + \frac{r^{i}}{(2i+1)\,a'^{i-1}}\,Y_{i}' + \dots\right)\right\}da'.$$

From this the attraction is readily obtained by differentiating with respect to r.

CHAPTER IV.

ATTRACTION OF BODIES NEITHER SPHERICAL NOR SPHEROIDAL, NOR NEARLY SO.

47. THE methods which have hitherto been given enable us to find the attraction of the Earth and other bodies of our system considered as a whole. But, taking the Earth as our example, the surface is irregular, and neither exactly spherical nor spheroidal. We ought, therefore, to be able to calculate the effect of these irregularities, and with this view the present Chapter is added to what has gone before. High Table-lands may very materially affect the position of the plumb-line in some places. Enormous irregular mountain masses, like the Himmalayas, may do the same. Their effect ought, therefore, to be carefully estimated, as all instruments which are fixed by the plumb-line or spirit-level must be affected by such irregularities.

PROP. *To find the attraction of a slender prism of matter on a point in the line drawn to one of its extremities.*

48. Let AB be the prism, C the attracted point, P any element of the prism, $AP = r$, M the mass and l the length of the prism, $AC = a$, $BC = b$, $PC = y$, angle $PAC = \theta$.

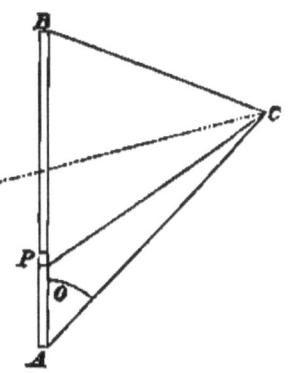

Then the mass of the element at $P = M\dfrac{dr}{l}$.

Attraction of element at P on $C = M\dfrac{dr}{l}\dfrac{1}{y^2}$.

Ditto in direction

$$CA = M\frac{dr}{l}\frac{1}{y^2}\cos PCA$$

$$= \frac{Mdr}{l} \frac{a - r \cos \theta}{y^3} \, , \quad y^2 = a^2 + r^2 - 2ar \cos \theta,$$

$$= \frac{Mdr}{l} \cdot \frac{a \sin^2 \theta - \cos \theta \, (r - a \cos \theta)}{[a^2 + r^2 - 2ar \cos \theta]^{\frac{3}{2}}} \, ;$$

∴ attraction of whole prism

$$= \frac{M}{l} \frac{r - a \cos \theta + a \cos \theta}{a \sqrt{a^2 + r^2 - 2ar \cos \theta}} \, , \text{ from } r = 0 \text{ to } r = l,$$

$$= \frac{M}{al} \frac{l}{\sqrt{a^2 + l^2 - 2al \cos \theta}} = \frac{M}{ab} \, .$$

As this is symmetrical with respect to a and b, it shows that the particle is attracted equally towards the two extremities of the prism; and that therefore the resultant attraction acts in a line bisecting the angle which the prism subtends at the attracted point.

PROP. *To find the attraction of a slender pyramid of any form upon a particle at its vertex; and also of a frustum of the pyramid.*

49. Let l be the length of the pyramid, a the area of a transverse section at distance unity from the vertex; r the distance of any section; ar^2 is its area; ρ the density of the matter: then $ar^2\rho dr$ is the mass of an element of the pyramid, and this divided by r^2 is its attraction;

∴ attraction of pyramid on vertex $= \int_0^l a\rho \, dr = a\rho l.$

If d is the length of any frustum of the pyramid, and $l = l' + d$, then

attraction of pyramid, length l', $= a\rho l'$;

∴ attraction of frustum $= a\rho d.$

It is observable that this is quite independent of the distance of the frustum from the vertex; and therefore all portions of the pyramid of equal length, any where selected, attract the vertex equally.

50. COR. Suppose the angular *width* of the pyramid to be β and to remain constant, while the angular depth varies; and let k be the linear depth of the transverse section of the base; then $a\beta l k$ is the area of the base; and the attraction of the whole pyramid on the vertex $= \rho\beta k$. Hence, all pyramids having the same angular width and the same linear depth at the base attract their vertex alike, whatever their lengths be.

PROP. *To find the attraction of an extensive circular plain of given depth or thickness upon a station above its middle point.*

51. Let t be the thickness or depth; h the height of the particle from the nearer surface, c the radius, r the radius of any intermediate elementary annulus of the attracting mass, z its depth. The several elements of this annulus of matter will attract the particle towards the plain equally. Hence attraction of the particle

$$= \int_0^t \int_0^c \frac{2\pi\rho r\,(h+z)\,dr\,dz}{[r^2+(h+z)^2]^{\frac{3}{2}}} = \int_0^c 2\pi\rho \left\{ \text{const.} - \frac{r}{\sqrt{r^2+(h+z)^2}} \right\} dr$$

$$= 2\pi\rho \int_0^c \left\{ \frac{r}{\sqrt{r^2+h^2}} - \frac{r}{\sqrt{r^2+(h+t)^2}} \right\} dr$$

$$= 2\pi\rho \left[\sqrt{c^2+h^2} - h - \sqrt{c^2+(h+t)^2} + h + t \right]$$

$$= 2\pi\rho \left[t - \sqrt{c^2+h^2} \left\{ \left(1 + \frac{2ht+t^2}{c^2+h^2} \right)^{\frac{1}{2}} - 1 \right\} \right]$$

$$= 2\pi\rho t \left\{ 1 - \frac{h+\frac{1}{2}t}{\sqrt{c^2+h^2}} + \dots \right\}.$$

52. If the plain be of infinite extent, the attraction equals $2\pi\rho t$; and this remarkable result is true, that it is independent of the distance from the plain. The same will be the case if the height of the station above the middle of the attracting

mass below, that is, $h + \frac{1}{2}t$, be so small that it may be neglected in comparison with the distance of the station from the furthest limit of the plain.

53. Ex. Suppose the height of the station above the middle of the mass below, that is, $h + \frac{1}{2}t$, is $\frac{1}{4}$ a mile and c 10 miles. Then the second term within the brackets is less than 0·05, and the attraction is very much the same as if the plain were unlimited in extent.

54. Cor. The result of this Proposition when the plain is unlimited in extent might have been foreseen from the result in the previous Proposition regarding the attraction of the frustum of a pyramid. Conceive an infinite number of slender pyramids to be drawn from the station intersecting the attracting plain; they will cut out of it an equal number of frustra, and the cosines of the angles they make with the perpendicular to the plain will be the thickness divided by the lengths of the frustra. But the attractions of the frustra are proportional to their lengths, and independent of the distance from the attracted point: (see Art. 49). Hence the resultant attraction of the whole will depend solely upon the thickness or depth of matter constituting the plain.

Prop. *To find the attraction of a rectangular mass, of small elevation compared with its length and breadth, upon a point lying in the plane of one of its larger sides.*

55. Let the attracted point be the origin of co-ordinates; the axes of x and y parallel to the long edges of the tabular mass, the axis of z being measured upwards. Let $x'y'z'$ be the co-ordinates to any point of the mass: xy co-ordinates to the nearest angle, XY to the furthest angle, H the height of the mass; ρ the density, supposed the same throughout.

Then $\rho\, dx'dy'dz'$ is the mass of the element; and the height being small, we may suppose the element projected on the plane of xy. Hence the whole attraction parallel to x

$$= \rho \int_x^X \int_y^Y \int_0^H \frac{x'\,dx'dy'dz'}{[x'^2+y'^2]^{\frac{3}{2}}} = \rho\, H \int_x^X \int_y^Y \frac{x'\,dx'dy'}{[x'^2+y'^2]^{\frac{3}{2}}}$$

$$= \rho \Pi \int_{s}^{x} \left\{ \frac{Y}{\sqrt{x'^2 + Y^2}} - \frac{y}{\sqrt{x'^2 + y^2}} \right\} \frac{dx'}{x'}$$

$$= \rho \Pi \log_{\epsilon} \left[\frac{\sqrt{1 + \frac{Y^2}{x^2}} + \frac{Y}{x}}{\sqrt{1 + \frac{Y^2}{X^2}} + \frac{Y}{X}} \cdot \frac{\sqrt{1 + \frac{y^2}{X^2}} + \frac{y}{X}}{\sqrt{1 + \frac{y^2}{x^2}} + \frac{y}{x}} \right].$$

To simplify the formula put

$$\frac{Y}{x} = \tan \theta_1, \quad \frac{y}{X} = \tan \theta_2, \quad \frac{Y}{X} = \tan \theta_3, \quad \frac{y}{x} = \tan \theta_4;$$

$$\therefore \sqrt{1 + \frac{Y^2}{x^2}} + \frac{Y}{x} = \frac{1 + \sin \theta_1}{\cos \theta_1} = \tan (45° + \tfrac{1}{2}\theta_1),$$

and so of the rest. Hence, since 0·434 is the modulus of common logarithms,

$$\text{attraction} = \frac{\rho H}{0·434} \left\{ \log \tan (45° + \tfrac{1}{2}\theta_1) + \log \tan (45° + \tfrac{1}{2}\theta_2) \right.$$

$$\left. - \log \tan (45° + \tfrac{1}{2}\theta_3) - \log \tan (45° + \tfrac{1}{2}\theta_4) \right\},$$

which gives a remarkably simple rule for finding the attraction parallel to x: that parallel to y can be found in like manner.

It is easy to show, that if the density be half the mean density of the earth, that is, about the same as granite, g be gravity, the radius of the earth = 20923713 feet, and H be expressed in feet, the coefficient above $= \dfrac{gH}{76127500}$.

This equals $gH \tan \left(\dfrac{1''}{569} \right)$. Hence, since the tangent of deflexion of the plumb-line caused by the attraction equals, by the parallelogram of forces, the ratio of the attraction to gravity, and the angle is very small,

Deflexion of plumb-line caused by the Tabular Mass parallel to the axis of x

$$= \frac{1''}{569} \, H \left\{ \log \tan (45^\circ + \tfrac{1}{2}\theta_{\shortmid}) + \log \tan (45^\circ + \tfrac{1}{2}\theta_{\shortparallel}) \right.$$

$$\left. - \log \tan (45^\circ + \tfrac{1}{2}\theta_{\shortmid}) - \log \tan (45^\circ + \tfrac{1}{2}\theta_{\shortparallel}) \right\}.$$

It is evident that the Tabular Mass may be partly below and partly above the plane of xy, so long as the height or depth is not so great that its square may not be neglected in comparison with the square of the distance from the attracted point. In this case H is the sum of the height and depth, above and below the plane of xy.

56. **Ex. 1.** The co-ordinates to the nearest and furthest angles of a tabular block of rock measured from the attracted point are 3 and -16, 40 and 30 miles, and the height of the mass from bottom to top is 628 feet. Show that the deflexion of the plumb-line parallel to the shorter side of the parallelogram $= 3''\cdot 172$.

Ex. 2. A table-land 1610 feet high, commencing at a distance of 20 miles from Takal K'hera, near the Great Arc of Meridian in India, runs 80 miles north, and 60 miles to the east and 60 to the west. Find the deviation of the plumb-line at that station. It is about $5''$; so considerable as materially to affect the Survey operations, and to have rendered it necessary to abandon that place as a principal station.

In cases where the attracting mass is near, it is necessary to cut it up into prisms and calculate the effect of each separately and add the results. Examples of this are seen in the celebrated case of Schehallien, and more recently in the calculation of the deflexion at Arthur's Seat, Edinburgh, by Lieut. Colonel James, Superintendent of the Ordnance Survey. See *Philosophical Transactions* for 1856, p. 591.

57. The irregular character of the surface of the Earth over large tracts of country, consisting of mountain and valley and ocean, may in some instances have a sensible effect, by presenting an excess or deficiency of attracting matter, upon the position of the plumb-line, in such a way as to derange delicate Survey operations. Hindostan affords a remarkable example of this, as the most extensive and the highest

mountain-ground in the world lies to the north of that continent, and an unbroken expanse of ocean stretches south down to the south pole. Both these causes, by opposite effects, make the plumb-line hang somewhat northerly of the true vertical.

In the following Propositions a method is laid down for calculating the attraction of an irregular superficial stratum of the Earth's surface, and making it depend altogether upon the contour of the surface. The method pursued is this: A law of geometric dissection of the surface is discovered which divides it into a number of four-sided spaces, such that if the height of the attracting mass were the same in them all, they would all attract the given station exactly to the same amount, whether far or near. In this case it would be necessary only to calculate for one space, then count the number of spaces in the country under consideration, and the final result is easily attained. The country being supposed irregular, the heights in the spaces will not be all alike. The principle, therefore, should be stated thus, that the attractions of the masses on the several compartments are in proportion to their mean heights. These mean heights are known by knowing the contour of the country.

-PROP. *To discover a Law of Dissection of the surface of the earth into compartments, so that the attractions of the masses of matter standing on them, upon a given station, shall be exactly proportional to the mean heights of the masses, be they far or near.*

58. Suppose a number of great circles to be drawn from the station in question to the antipodes, making any angle β, each with the next, thus dividing the earth's surface (which we may in this calculation suppose to be a sphere, without incurring any sensible error) into a number of Lunes. Then, with the station as centre, describe on the surface a number of circles, at distances the law of which it is our object now to determine, dividing the whole into a number of four-sided compartments.

We will begin by calculating the attraction of a mass of matter, standing on one of these compartments, at a uniform height throughout, upon the station in a horizontal direction.

P. A.   4

Let a and $a + \phi$ be the angular distances from the station of the two circles bounding this compartment; h the height of the mass; θ the angular distance along the surface of an elementary vertical prism of the mass; a the radius of the earth; ψ the angle which the plane of θ makes with the plane of the mid-line of the lune, and in which latter plane the resultant attraction evidently acts. The area of the base of the prism $= a^2 \sin \theta \, d\psi \, d\theta$.

Since the height of prism (h) is supposed very small, the distances of its two extremities from the station may be taken to be the same, and $= 2a \sin \frac{1}{2}\theta$. Its attraction along the chord of θ, by Art. 48,

$$= \frac{\rho a^2 h \sin \theta \, d\theta \, d\psi}{4 a^2 \sin^2 \frac{1}{2}\theta}.$$

Attraction along the tangent to $\theta = \dfrac{\rho h \sin \theta \, d\theta \, d\psi}{4 \sin^2 \frac{1}{2}\theta} \cos \frac{1}{2}\theta$;

$\therefore$ attraction along the tangent to the mid-line of the lune

$$= \frac{\rho h \cos^2 \frac{1}{2}\theta \, d\theta \, d\psi}{2 \sin \frac{1}{2}\theta} \cos \psi \, ;$$

$\therefore$ attraction of the whole mass

$$= \frac{\rho h}{2} \int_a^{a+\phi} \int_{-\frac{1}{2}\beta}^{\frac{1}{2}\beta} \frac{\cos^2 \frac{1}{2}\theta}{\sin \frac{1}{2}\theta} \, d\theta \, . \, \cos \psi \, d\psi$$

$$= \rho h \sin \frac{1}{2}\beta \int_a^{a+\phi} \frac{\cos^2 \frac{1}{2}\theta}{\sin \frac{1}{2}\theta} \, d\theta$$

$$= 2\rho h \sin \frac{1}{2}\beta \left[\log_e \frac{\tan \frac{1}{4}(a + \phi)}{\tan \frac{1}{4}a} + \cos \frac{1}{2}(a + \phi) - \cos \frac{1}{2}a \right]$$

$$= 2\rho h \sin \frac{1}{2}\beta \left[\log_e \frac{\sin(\frac{1}{4}a + \frac{1}{4}\phi) + \sin \frac{1}{4}\phi}{\sin(\frac{1}{4}a + \frac{1}{4}\phi) - \sin \frac{1}{4}\phi} - 2\sin(\frac{1}{2}a + \frac{1}{4}\phi) \sin \frac{1}{4}\phi \right]$$

$$= 4\rho h \sin \frac{1}{2}\beta \sin \frac{1}{4}\phi \left\{ \frac{1}{\sin(\frac{1}{4}a + \frac{1}{4}\phi)} - \sin(\frac{1}{2}a + \frac{1}{4}\phi) \right\}$$

neglecting only the cube and higher powers of sin $\frac{1}{2}\phi$,

$$= \rho h \sin \tfrac{1}{2}\beta \cdot \frac{\phi \cos^2(\tfrac{1}{2}a + \tfrac{1}{4}\phi)}{\sin(\tfrac{1}{2}a + \tfrac{1}{4}\phi)}, \text{ neglecting } \phi^2 \text{ &c.}$$

The law of dissection we shall choose will simplify this; for we are to assume such a relation between ϕ and a that the expression in ϕ may be constant, in order to make the attraction the same for all compartments in which h is the same or varying as h where the heights of the masses standing on the compartments are different. As the value of the constant to which we equal the function of a and ϕ is quite arbitrary, we will assume it such that when a and ϕ are small, ϕ shall

$$= \tfrac{1}{10}a \text{ In this case it} = \frac{\tfrac{1}{10}a}{\tfrac{1}{2}a + \tfrac{1}{40}a} = \frac{4}{21}.$$

Hence
$$\frac{\phi \cos^2(\tfrac{1}{2}a + \tfrac{1}{4}\phi)}{\sin(\tfrac{1}{2}a + \tfrac{1}{4}\phi)} = \frac{4}{21} \dots\dots\dots\dots (1),$$

defines the Law of Dissection.

The attraction of the mass standing on the compartment, in consequence,

$$= \frac{4}{21} \rho h \sin \tfrac{1}{2}\beta;$$

an exceedingly simple expression. We may obtain it in terms of gravity as follows. Let ρ the density be the same as that of the mountain Schehallien, viz. 2.75; the mean density, according to Mr Baily's repetition of the Cavendish experiment, being 5.66; g gravity; $a = 4000$ miles.

Now $g = \frac{4\pi}{3} a \times$ mean density $= \frac{4\pi}{3} a \frac{566}{275} \rho$;

$\therefore$ attraction of mass on any compartment

$$= \frac{4}{12} \frac{3}{4\pi} \frac{275}{566} \frac{h}{a} g = 0.000005523 h \sin \tfrac{1}{2}\beta.g,$$

being expressed in parts of a mile.

Since $0.000005523 = \tan(1''.1392)$;

∴ deflection of the plumb-line caused by this attraction

$$= 1''.1392\lambda \sin \tfrac{1}{2}\beta \quad\ldots\ldots\ldots\ldots\ldots\ldots\quad (2).$$

The method of using this theorem is as follows. When the numerical values of the successive pairs of α and ϕ are determined by the solution of equation (1) giving the law of dissection, lay them and the lunes down on a map of the country the attraction of which is to be found. It will thus be covered with compartments. After examining the map, write down the average heights of the masses standing on all the several compartments of any one lune; add them together, multiply the sum by $1''.1392 \sin \tfrac{1}{2}\beta$, and equation (2) shows that we have the deflection caused by the mass on the whole lune in the vertical plane of its middle line. Multiply by the cosine and then the sine of the azimuth of that middle line, and we have the deflections in the meridian and the prime-vertical. The same being done for all the lunes, and the results added, we have the effects in meridian and prime-vertical produced by the whole country under consideration.

59. Cor. That the mass on each compartment will attract as if collected at the middle of the mid-line appears from what follows. Let Θ be the distance at which the matter may be concentrated so as to produce the same effect as the actual mass. Now the area of the compartment

$$= \int_{\alpha}^{\alpha+\phi}\int_{-\frac{1}{2}\beta}^{\frac{1}{2}\beta} a^2 \sin\theta\, d\theta\, d\psi = a^2\beta \int_{\alpha}^{\alpha+\phi} \sin\theta\, d\theta$$

$$= a^2\beta\,[\cos\alpha - \cos(\alpha+\phi)] = 2a^2\beta \sin\tfrac{1}{2}\phi \sin(\alpha + \tfrac{1}{2}\phi).$$

Then by the last Proposition,

$$\rho h \sin\tfrac{1}{2}\beta\, \frac{\phi \cos^2(\tfrac{1}{2}\alpha + \tfrac{1}{4}\phi)}{\sin(\tfrac{1}{2}\alpha + \tfrac{1}{4}\phi)} = \text{attraction, by hypothesis}$$

$$= \rho h\, \frac{2a^2\beta \sin\tfrac{1}{2}\phi \sin(\alpha + \tfrac{1}{2}\phi)}{4a^2 \sin^2\tfrac{1}{2}\Theta}\, \cos\tfrac{1}{2}\Theta\,;$$

$$\therefore \frac{\sin^2 \frac{1}{2}\Theta}{\cos \frac{1}{2}\Theta} = \frac{\frac{1}{2}\beta}{\sin \frac{1}{2}\beta} \frac{\sin \frac{1}{2}\phi}{\frac{1}{2}\phi} \frac{\sin^2 (\frac{1}{2}a + \frac{1}{4}\phi)}{\cos (\frac{1}{2}a + \frac{1}{4}\phi)} \cdot$$

Hence, if β be not taken larger than 30°, and since ϕ is always small, this gives $\Theta = a + \frac{1}{2}\phi$, which coincides with the middle of the mid-line of the compartment.

PROP. *To calculate the dimensions of the successive compartments from the law of dissection.*

60. For this purpose we should solve the equation of last Proposition, viz.

$$\frac{\phi \cos^2 (\frac{1}{2}a + \frac{1}{4}\phi)}{\sin (\frac{1}{2}a + \frac{1}{4}\phi)} = \frac{4}{21} \quad \ldots\ldots\ldots\ldots (1).$$

But this cannot be done. We must therefore approximate, which will equally well suit our purpose. In order to afford a test of the values we arrive at the equation may be written under the following form. Putting the angle ϕ for the arc ϕ,

$$\phi^\circ = \frac{4}{21} \frac{180}{\pi} \frac{\sin (\frac{1}{2}a + \frac{1}{4}\phi)}{\cos^2 (\frac{1}{2}a + \frac{1}{4}\phi)} ;$$

$$\text{or} = \log^{-1} \left\{ \begin{array}{l} 11.0379639 \\ + \log \sin (\frac{1}{2}a + \frac{1}{4}\phi) \\ - 2 \log \cos (\frac{1}{2}a + \frac{1}{4}\phi) \end{array} \right\} \ldots\ldots\ldots\ldots (3).$$

Equation (1) can be solved by expansion so long as a and ϕ are not too large.

It gives

$$\phi = \frac{4}{21} \left(\frac{a}{2} + \frac{\phi}{4}\right) \left\{ 1 - \frac{1}{6} \left(\frac{a}{2} + \frac{\phi}{4}\right)^2 + \left(\frac{a}{2} + \frac{\phi}{4}\right)^2 \right\}$$

$$= \frac{2}{21} \left(a + \frac{\phi}{2}\right) \left\{ 1 + \frac{5}{6} \left(\frac{a}{2} + \frac{\phi}{4}\right)^2 \right\} ;$$

$$\therefore \frac{a}{\phi} + \frac{1}{2} = \frac{21}{2} \left\{ 1 - \frac{5}{6} \left(\frac{a}{2} + \frac{\phi}{4}\right)^2 \right\},$$

$$\frac{a}{\phi} = 10\left\{1 - \frac{7}{8}\left(\frac{a}{2} + \frac{\phi}{4}\right)^2\right\},$$

$$\frac{\phi}{a} = \frac{1}{10}\left\{1 + \frac{7}{8}\left(\frac{a}{2} + \frac{\phi}{4}\right)^2\right\} = \frac{1}{10}\left\{1 + \frac{7}{8}\left(\frac{a}{2} + \frac{a}{40}\right)^2\right\}$$

$$= \frac{1}{10}\left(1 + 0.2411a^2\right),$$

or, if a be expressed in degrees,

$$= \frac{1}{10}\left(1 + 0.000073a^2\right) \quad\dots\dots\dots\dots\dots\dots\dots\dots\dots \text{(4)}.$$

Let $a_1 a_2 a_3 \dots \phi_1 \phi_2 \phi_3 \dots$ be the successive values of a and ϕ for the several compartments of a lune. These are connected by the following relations:

$$a_2 = a_1 + \phi_1, \quad a_3 = a_2 + \phi_2, \dots\dots$$

Suppose that for the first compartment $a_1 = 0°.75$[*], then

[*] This particular value is here used because the calculations following are taken from a Paper, by the author, in the *Philosophical Transactions* for 1855, upon Himmalayan Attraction, and three-fourths of a degree is about the distance of the nearest hills from the northern station of the Great Indian Arc of Meridian. Any other value for a_1 might have been taken. The results above deduced are perfectly general, and are applicable to any other similar problem. If compartments with elevations or depressions occur in the map, nearer to the station than three-fourths of a degree, or about 52 miles, their dimensions can easily be calculated backwards, i.e. towards the station, by the help of the formula

$$\phi_{-n} = \frac{1}{10}a_{-n} = \frac{1}{11}a_{-n+1}, \text{ since } a_{-n+1} = a_{-n} + \phi_{-n}.$$

The succeeding values, reckoning from a_1 and ϕ_1 are here given, as they may be of use for reference.

a_1 = 0°.75	ϕ_1 = 0°.075		a_{-9} = 0°.28	ϕ_{-9} = 0°.028
a_0 = 0.68	ϕ_0 = 0.068		a_{-10} = 0.25	ϕ_{-10} = 0.025
a_{-1} = 0.62	ϕ_{-1} = 0.062		a_{-11} = 0.23	ϕ_{-11} = 0.023
a_{-2} = 0.56	ϕ_{-2} = 0.056		a_{-12} = 0.21	ϕ_{-12} = 0.021
a_{-3} = 0.51	ϕ_{-3} = 0.051		a_{-13} = 0.19	ϕ_{-13} = 0.019
a_{-4} = 0.46	ϕ_{-4} = 0.046		a_{-14} = 0.17	ϕ_{-14} = 0.017
a_{-5} = 0.42	ϕ_{-5} = 0.042		a_{-15} = 0.15	ϕ_{-15} = 0.015
a_{-6} = 0.38	ϕ_{-6} = 0.038		a_{-16} = 0.14	ϕ_{-16} = 0.014
a_{-7} = 0.34	ϕ_{-7} = 0.034		a_{-17} = 0.13	ϕ_{-17} = 0.013
a_{-8} = 0.31	ϕ_{-8} = 0.031		&c.	&c.

by (4) $\phi_1 = 0°.075$; therefore $a_2 = 0°.825$: and by proceeding in this way we obtain the following pairs of values by this formula.

$a_1 = 0°.75$	$\phi_1 = 0°.075$	$a_{22} = 5°.55$	$\phi_{22} = 0°.555$
$c_2 = 0.83$	$\phi_2 = 0.083$	$a_{23} = 6.11$	$\phi_{23} = 0.611$
$a_3 = 0.91$	$\phi_3 = 0.091$	$a_{24} = 6.72$	$\phi_{24} = 0.672$
$a_4 = 1.00$	$\phi_4 = 0.100$	$a_{25} = 7.39$	$\phi_{25} = 0.739$
$c_5 = 1.10$	$\phi_5 = 0.110$	$c_{26} = 8.13$	$\phi_{26} = 0.813$
$a_6 = 1.21$	$\phi_6 = 0.121$	$a_{27} = 8.94$	$\phi_{27} = 0.894$
$a_7 = 1.33$	$\phi_7 = 0.133$	$a_{28} = 9.83$	$\phi_{28} = 0.983$
$\sigma_8 = 1.46$	$\phi_8 = 0.146$	$a_{29} = 10.82$	$\phi_{29} = 1.089$
$a_9 = 1.61$	$\phi_9 = 0.161$	$a_{30} = 11.91$	$\phi_{30} = 1.202$
$a_{10} = 1.77$	$\phi_{10} = 0.177$	$a_{31} = 13.11$	$\phi_{31} = 1.326$
$o_{11} = 1.95$	$\phi_{11} = 0.195$	$a_{32} = 14.43$	$\phi_{32} = 1.462$
$a_{12} = 2.14$	$\phi_{12} = 0.214$	$a_{33} = 15.99$	$\phi_{33} = 1.620$
$a_{13} = 2.35$	$\phi_{13} = 0.235$	$a_{34} = 17.61$	$\phi_{34} = 1.800$
$a_{14} = 2.59$	$\phi_{14} = 0.259$	$a_{35} = 19.41$	$\phi_{35} = 1.992$
$a_{15} = 2.85$	$\phi_{15} = 0.285$	$a_{36} = 21.40$	$\phi_{36} = 2.211$
$a_{16} = 3.13$	$\phi_{16} = 0.313$	$a_{37} = 23.61$	$\phi_{37} = 2.456$
$a_{17} = 3.45$	$\phi_{17} = 0.345$	$a_{38} = 26.06$	$\phi_{38} = 2.732$
$c_{18} = 3.79$	$\phi_{18} = 0.379$	$a_{39} = 28.79$	$\phi_{39} = 3.054$
$a_{19} = 4.17$	$\phi_{19} = 0.417$	$c_{40} = 31.84$	$\phi_{40} = 3.419$
$a_{20} = 4.59$	$\phi_{20} = 0.459$	$c_{41} = 35.26$	$\phi_{41} = 3.600$
$a_{21} = 5.05$	$\phi_{21} = 0.505$	$a_{42} = 38.86$	$\phi_{42} = 4.314$

That these results derived from the approximate formula (4) are thus far correct, we gather from the fact that the last pair, viz. $a_{42} = 38°.86$ and $\phi_{42} = 4°.314$ sufficiently satisfy the test (3) when substituted. Beyond this pair, we cannot use (4), but must solve equation (1), or rather (3), by trial. This leads to the following pairs of values stretching to the antipodes.

$a_{43} = 43°.17$	$\phi_{43} = 4°.980$	$a_{47} = 68°.94$	$\phi_{47} = 10°.380$
$a_{44} = 48.15$	$\phi_{44} = 5.783$	$a_{48} = 79.27$	$\phi_{48} = 14.030$
$a_{45} = 53.98$	$\phi_{45} = 6.800$	$a_{49} = 93.30$	$\phi_{49} = 23.380$
$a_{46} = 60.73$	$\phi_{46} = 8.210$	$a_{50} = 116.68$	ϕ_{50} imperfect.

61.   The formulæ here deduced may be applied to find the effect on the plumb-line of any mountain-region, or hollow (as in the case of the ocean), so long as the angle subtended at the station by any part of it is such as to allow its square to be neglected

In the *Philosophical Transactions* for 1855 and 1858-9, the author has applied these principles to find the effect of the Himmalayas and the mountain-region beyond them on the plumb-line in India, and has found that the meridian deflection caused in the northern station of the Great Arc of Meridian (lat. 29° 30′ 48″, and long. 77° 42′) is nearly 28″, as far as the data regarding the contour of the mass can be ascertained; and that the astronomical amplitudes between that and the next principal station (lat. 24° 7′ 11″), and between that and the third (lat. 18° 3′ 15″), are diminished by the quantities 15″.9 and 5″.3.   He has also shown that the meridian deflection between the first and third of these stations varies very nearly inversely as the distance from a point in the meridian in latitude 33° 30′.

62.   The effect of the deficiency of matter in the Ocean south of Hindostan down to the south pole is also calculated, upon an assumed but not improbable law of the depth, and found to produce a meridian deflection northwards at the three stations specified of about 6″, 9″, 10″.5 respectively; and 19″.7 at Cape Comorin.

63.   It is possible that, the superabundant matter in mountain-regions having been heaved up from below, there may be a deficiency of matter below the mountains which would under certain circumstances have the tendency of counteracting their effect on the plumb-line.   This Mr Airy has suggested in a Paper in the *Philosophical Transactions* of 1855, on the hypothesis that the deficiency is immediately below the mountains close to their mass.   Upon the supposition that the mountains may have drawn their mass from the regions below through a considerable depth, by an extensive and small expansion of the matter in those lower regions, the author has calculated the modifying effect on the plumb-

line in the *Transactions* for 1858-9.   This has brought to light
the fact, that a trifling deviation in the density from that
required for fluid-equilibrium, if it prevail through extensive
tracts, may have a sensible effect upon the plumb-line.   The
following Proposition, with which we shall close this Chapter,
will show this.   These questions, in themselves interesting as
problems in Attraction, become still more so, as we shall see,
in the determination of the Figure of the Earth.

Prop.   *To find the effect on the plumb-line of a slight but
wide-spread deviation in density in the interior of the earth,
either in excess or defect, from that required by the laws of
fluid-equilibrium.*

64.   Suppose vertical lines drawn down through the four
angles of any compartment to a depth d, and a surface uniting
the four extremities drawn, so as to form the frustum of a
pyramid of which the vertex is in the centre of the earth:
draw also a vertical line of length d through the mid-point of
the compartment.   Suppose the height of the matter standing
on the compartment to be uniform and equal to one mile.
Let the several vertical prisms of which it consists be conceived to be distributed downwards uniformly through the
depth d, the density of this lengthened prism will be less
than that of the superficial rock in the ratio of $1 : d$.   Let u
and v be the distances of the extremities of this long prism
from the station.   Then the attraction of the short prism
along the chord of the surface $= \dfrac{\text{mass}}{u^2}$, and (by Art. 48) that

of the longer $= \dfrac{\text{mass}}{uv}$.   Hence along the horizontal line at the

station $\dfrac{\text{attraction of slender prism}}{\text{attraction of the prism at surface}} = \dfrac{u}{v}$.

Now in Art. 59, it has been shown that the attracting mass
on any compartment may be considered concentrated in the
mid-point.   Much more may this be done with the horizontal
layers of the frustum which are not of larger dimensions than
the compartment, and are farther off from the station.   Hence
if u_1 and v_1 be the distances from the station of the extremities

of the vertical line d through the middle point of the mid-line of the compartment, the attraction of the mass on the compartment, and the deflection caused by it, must both be diminished in the ratio of u_1 to v_1 to find the effect of the same mass distributed through a depth d. Suppose the masses (one mile high) on n compartments of any lune are thus distributed; then by Art. 58, formula (2),

$$\text{Deflexion} = 1''.1392 \sin \tfrac{1}{2}\beta \left\{\frac{u_1}{v_1} + \frac{u_2}{v_2} + \ldots\ldots + \frac{u_n}{v_n}\right\}.$$

If $\beta = 30°$, the coefficient $= 1''.1392 \times 0.258 = 0''.294$.

65. We will take an example. Let the width of the lune $\beta = 30°$, and let the 21 compartments from a_1 to a_{21} (see Table in Art. 60) be included. This will be a tract of country $5°.55 - 0°.75 = 4°.8$, or 334 miles in length, and the breadth at the mid-point will $= \sin \tfrac{1}{2} (5°.55 + 0°.75) \times$ the length of $30° = 0.055 \times 30 \times 69.5 = 114$ miles; and, by spherical trigonometry, the area is, in round numbers, 38,500 square miles. We will take three examples of depth which (for convenience of calculation) we will express in the length of degrees, viz. $3°$, $6°$, and $9°$; which nearly equal 208, 417, and 625 miles. The vertical thicknesses of these three divisions of the frustum are each $= 3° = 208$ miles. The widths, however, parallel to the horizon grow less in passing downwards. But owing to the convergency of the radii bounding the elementary prisms, the density increases in the distribution of the matter in exactly the same proportion that the area of the horizontal section diminishes. The amount of matter in the three divisions is therefore the same, and we may consider the volumes the same, and each equal to $38,500 \times 208 = 8,008,000$ cubic miles $= 3\text{-}100,000$th parts of the volume of the whole earth.

Now since the greatest of $u_1 u_2 \ldots u_n$ is less than $6°$, we may take the arc for the chord without sensible error. Then, with respect to all these quantities, $\dfrac{u}{v} =$ the cosine of the angle of which $\dfrac{u}{d}$ is the cotangent. This enables us without difficulty with the help of a Table of cosines and co-tangents to form the sum of the series in the last Article. The values of u are the first 21 values of a in the Table in Art. 60.

$d = 3°$		$d = 6°$		$d = 9°$	
$\frac{u}{d} = \cot$	$\cos = \frac{u}{v}$	$\frac{u}{d} = \cot$	$\cos = \frac{u}{v}$	$\frac{u}{d} = \cot$	$\cos = \frac{u}{v}$
0.250	0.242	0.125	0.124	0.083	0.083
0.277	0.267	0.138	0.137	0.092	0.092
0.303	0.290	0.152	0.150	0.101	0.100
0.333	0.316	0.166	0.164	0.111	0.110
0.367	0.344	0.184	0.181	0.122	0.121
0.403	0.374	0.201	0.197	0.134	0.133
0.443	0.405	0.222	0.217	0.148	0.146
0.487	0.438	0.243	0.236	0.162	0.160
0.537	0.473	0.269	0.260	0.179	0.176
0.590	0.508	0.295	0.283	0.197	0.193
0.650	0.545	0.325	0.309	0.217	0.212
0.713	0.581	0.356	0.335	0.238	0.232
0.783	0.617	0.392	0.365	0.261	0.253
0.863	0.653	0.431	0.396	0.288	0.277
0.950	0.689	0.475	0.429	0.317	0.302
1.043	0.722	0.522	0.463	0.348	0.329
1.150	0.755	0.575	0.498	0.383	0.358
1.263	0.784	0.631	0.534	0.421	0.388
1.390	0.812	0.695	0.571	0.463	0.420
1.530	0.837	0.765	0.608	0.510	0.454
1.683	0.860	0.842	0.644	0.561	0.489
sums = 11.512		= 7.101		= 5.028	
multiply by					
0″.294 = 3″.385		= 2″.088		= 1″.478	

From this Table we gather, that the Deflections caused at the station by the superficial mass one mile thick, when distributed uniformly through the depths 208, 417, 625 miles, are 3″.385, 2″.088, 1″.478. The densities of the matter thus diffused in these three cases are about $\frac{1}{200}$th, $\frac{1}{400}$th, $\frac{1}{600}$th of the density of the superficial rock. If we multiply the above deflections by 2, 4, 6, we have the deflections caused by matter, of 1-100th the density of superficial rock, distributed over the three depths, equal to 6".770, 8".352, 8".868. Retaining the first, subtracting the first from the second, and the second from the third, we have the three deflections caused by a mass of 208 miles vertical thickness (occupying 3-100,000th parts of the volume of the whole earth and of density 1-100th part of the density of the surface) the centre of which is at depths 104, 312, 521 miles: they are 6".770, 1".582, 0".516. We may finally change the comparison between the density of this space, 3-100,000ths of the earth's volume, in its three situations, with the density of surface, to a comparison with the average density of the earth itself at the several depths at which the centre of the space lies.

If D be the density of the surface, a the radius of the earth, the usually received law of density of the interior, determined from the fluid-theory, is

$$\text{Density at depth } d = \frac{2aD}{a-d}\sin\left(\frac{5\pi}{6}\frac{a-d}{a}\right).$$

When $d = 100$, 300, 500 miles, this gives the densities

$$1.14D, \ 1.43D, \ 1.71D.$$

Multiplying the last angles by the ratios of these densities to D, we have finally the Deflections—caused by an excess or defect of matter, prevailing through a space equal to 3-100,000th parts of the volume of the earth, and 1-100th part of the earth's density at the centre of the space—equal 7".7, 2".3, and 0".9, the depths of the centre of the space being about 100, 300, 500 miles.

The form of the space in its three positions is shown in the diagram; viz. DG, FI, HK; and O, P, Q are their centres. The particular form arises from the manner in which the mass is dissected, so as to make the calculation feasible. The result serves to show the kind of effect which slight but extensive variations from the density of fluid-equilibrium in the hidden regions below may have upon the plumb-line: and we shall find the use of this when we come to consider the Figure of the Earth : (see Art. 98).

66. Had the width *DB* been equal to the middle width at *a*, so as to make the boundaries *BC, DE* parallel, the effect

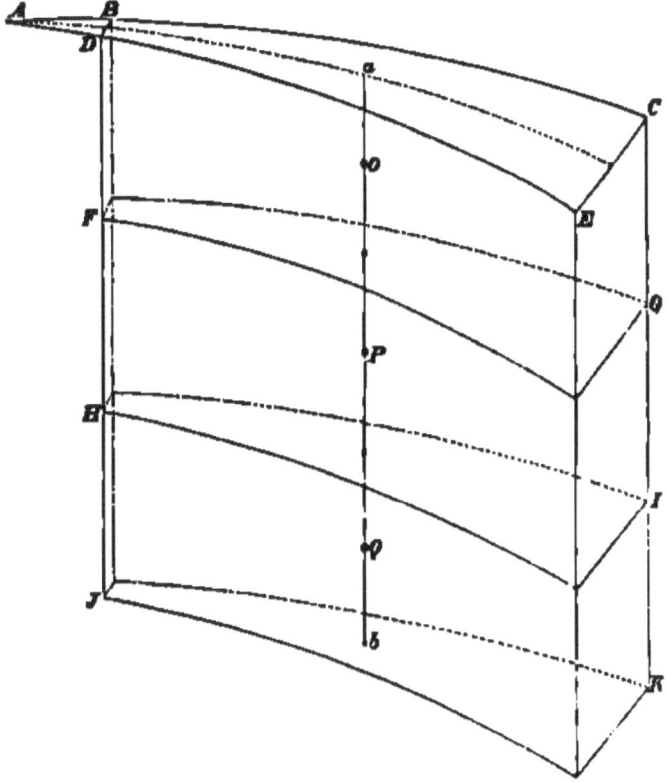

would have been very much greater. Moreover the defect or excess in density which we have taken, viz. 1-100th, might have been chosen larger, and the deflections proportionably increased. For there are many kinds of rock, as granite, which differ so in density in the different specimens that the difference between the extremes is greater even than 1-10th of the mean. And if this difference exists at the surface, it does not seem to be improper to suppose that great variations may exist also below, from the effect of the cooling down and solidifying of the crust, even much greater than 1-100th.

FIGURE OF THE EARTH.

CHAPTER I.

67. AFTER it was known that the earth is of a globular form, Newton was the first who demonstrated that it is not a perfect sphere. From theoretical considerations and also from the discovery that a pendulum moves slower at the equator than in higher latitudes, he arrived at the conclusion that its form is that of an oblate spheroid. This subject we propose to consider fully in the present Chapter, on the hypothesis that the Earth was a fluid mass when it assumed its present general form. The calculation is one of great difficulty, and would indeed be impracticable did we not know that the figure differs but little from a sphere.

As a first approximation we shall inquire whether a homogeneous fluid mass revolving about a fixed axis can be made to maintain a spheroidal form according to the laws of fluid pressure.

PROP. *A homogeneous mass of fluid in the form of a spheroid revolves with a uniform velocity about an axis: required to determine whether the equilibrium of the surface left free is possible.*

68. Let a and c be the semi-axes of the spheroid referred to three axes of rectangular co-ordinates, c being that about which it revolves: also let $c^2 = a^2 (1 - e^2)$. The forces which act upon the particle (xyz) are the centrifugal force and the attraction of the spheroid parallel to the axes: these latter are given in Art. 12, and are

$$\frac{2\pi\rho}{e^3}\left[\sqrt{1-e^2}\,\sin^{-1}e - e\,(1-e^2)\right]x,$$

$$\frac{2\pi\rho}{e^3}\left[\sqrt{1-e^2}\,\sin^{-1}e - e\,(1-e^2)\right]y,$$

$$\frac{4\pi\rho}{e^3}\left[e - \sqrt{1-e^2}\,\sin^{-1}e\right]z.$$

Let these be represented by Ax, By, Cz. Let ω be the angular velocity of the rotation, then $\omega^2\sqrt{x^2+y^2}$ is the centrifugal force of the particle (xyz), and the resolved parts of it parallel to the axes of x, y, z are ω^2x, ω^2y, 0. Hence X, Y, Z, the forces acting on (xyz) parallel to the axes, are

$$X = -(A-\omega^2)\,x, \quad Y = -(B-\omega^2)\,y, \quad Z = -Cz.$$

These make $Xdx + Ydy + Zdz$ a perfect differential, and therefore so far the equilibrium is possible.

The equation of fluid equilibrium gives

$$\frac{1}{\rho}\,dp = Xdx + Ydy + Zdz$$

$$= -(A-\omega^2)\,(xdx+ydy) - Czdz;$$

$$\therefore\ \frac{2p}{\rho} = \text{constant} - (A-\omega^2)\,(x^2+y^2) - Cz^2.$$

At the surface $p = 0$, and therefore

$$\frac{A-\omega^2}{C}\,(x^2+y^2) + z^2 = \text{const.}$$

is the equation to the surface; and this is a spheroid, and therefore the equilibrium is possible, the form of the spheroid being properly assumed. The eccentricity is given by the condition

$$1 - e^2 = \frac{c^2}{a^2} = \frac{A-\omega^2}{C},$$

or $\dfrac{\omega^2}{2\pi\rho} = \dfrac{\sqrt{1-e^2}}{e^3}\,\sin^{-1}e - 3\,\dfrac{1-e^2}{e^2} + \dfrac{2}{e^3}\,(1-e^2)^{\frac{1}{2}}\,\sin^{-1}e;$

$$\therefore \frac{w^2}{2\pi\rho} + 3\frac{1-e^2}{e^2} - \frac{(3-2e^2)\sqrt{1-e^2}}{e^3}\sin^{-1}e = 0.$$

Now observation shows that $\frac{1}{289}$ = the ratio of the centrifugal force at the equator to gravity at the equator. Hence

$$\frac{1}{289} = \frac{w^2 a}{\frac{4}{3}\pi\rho a - w^2 a}; \quad \therefore \frac{w^2}{2\pi\rho} = \frac{1}{435}.$$

By expanding in powers of e and neglecting powers higher than the second, because we know that the earth is nearly spherical, we have

$$\sin^{-1}e = e + \frac{1}{2}\frac{e^3}{3} + \frac{1.3}{2.4}\frac{e^5}{5} + \dots$$

$$\sqrt{1-e^2} = 1 - \frac{1}{2}e^2 - \frac{1.1}{2.4}e^4;$$

$$\therefore \frac{1}{435} = \left(\frac{3}{e^2} - 2\right)\left(1 - \frac{1}{2}e^2 - \frac{1}{8}e^4\right)\left(1 + \frac{1}{6}e^2 + \frac{3}{40}e^4\right) - \frac{3}{e^2} + 3$$

$$= \left(\frac{3}{e^2} - 2\right)\left(1 - \frac{1}{3}e^2 - \frac{2}{15}e^4\right) - \frac{3}{e^2} + 3 = \frac{4e^2}{15};$$

$$\therefore e^2 = \frac{1}{116}.$$

If e be the ellipticity, then

$$e = \frac{a-c}{a} = 1 - \sqrt{1-e^2} = \frac{1}{2}e^2 = \frac{1}{232}.$$

This result is so much greater than that obtained by other methods, as we shall see, that it decides against our considering the earth's mass to be homogeneous. Indeed it is *à priori* highly improbable that the mass should be homogeneous, since the pressure must increase in passing towards the centre and the matter be in consequence compressed.

69. Another value of e, nearly $= 1$, satisfies the equation. But this does not give the figure of any of the heavenly bodies, since none of them are very elliptical.

Since there are two values of e which satisfy the equation, it might be supposed that the equilibrium of the mass under one of these forms would be unstable, and, upon any derangement taking place, the fluid would pass to the other as a stable form. But Laplace has shown (*Méc. Céles.* Liv. III. § 21) that for a given primitive impulse there is but one form. In fact it is easily seen that for a given value of w, the angular velocity, the vis viva of two equal masses, so different in their form as to have e small and nearly equal unity, must be very different, and that therefore the mass cannot pass from one form to the other without a new impulse from without being given to its parts.

70. The relation between w and e in Art. 68, shows that as w alters e alters, and vice versâ. By putting $\dfrac{dw}{de} = 0$, we find the greatest value of w which is consistent with equilibrium. This after some long numerical calculations gives

$$e = \cdot\frac{17197}{27197}, \text{ and time of rotation} = 0\cdot1009 \text{ day.}$$

71. Before proceeding to calculate the ellipticity on the hypothesis of the earth's mass being heterogeneous we will take the following extreme case. The density increases as we pass down towards the centre. Suppose that at the centre it is infinitely greater than elsewhere: that is, suppose the whole force resides in the centre. The case of nature must lie between this hypothesis and that of the earth's being homogeneous.

PROP. *To calculate the ellipticity of a mass of fluid revolving about a fixed axis and attracted by a force residing wholly in the centre of the fluid and varying inversely as the square of the distance.*

72. Let M be the mass of the fluid; the other quantities as before;

$$\therefore\; X = -\frac{Mx}{r^3} + w^2 x, \quad Y = -\frac{My}{r^3} + w^2 y, \quad Z = -\frac{Mz}{r^3}.$$

Then the equation $Xdx + Ydy + Zdz = 0$ becomes

$$\frac{M}{r^3}(xdx + ydy + zdz) - w^2(xdx + ydy) = 0;$$

$$\therefore\; \frac{M}{r^3}dr - \frac{w^2}{2}d(x^2 + y^2) = 0;$$

$$\therefore\; \frac{M}{r} + \frac{w^2}{2}(x^2 + y^2) = \text{constant} = C.$$

Then $\qquad \dfrac{1}{289} = \dfrac{w^2 a}{\dfrac{M}{a^2} - w^2 a}, \quad \therefore\; \dfrac{M}{w^2 a^3} = 290;$

$$\therefore\; \frac{1}{r} \text{ or } \frac{1}{\sqrt{x^2 + y^2 + z^2}} = \frac{C}{M} - \frac{1}{580}\frac{x^2 + y^2}{a^3}.$$

By reversing this, squaring, expanding, and neglecting the square of $\dfrac{1}{580}$, this is seen to be the equation to a spheroid.

When $x=0$ and $y=0$, then $z = c$; when $z = 0$, $x^2 + y^2 = a^2$;

$$\therefore\; \frac{1}{c} = \frac{C}{M}, \; \frac{1}{a} = \frac{C}{M} - \frac{1}{580}\frac{1}{a}, \; \frac{c}{a} = \frac{580}{581};$$

$$\therefore\; \epsilon = \frac{1}{581}.$$

This value of ϵ is too small (as we might have expected), as $\dfrac{1}{232}$ is too large, to agree with the form deduced in other ways.

PROP. *To find the equation of equilibrium of a heterogeneous mass of fluid consisting of strata each nearly spherical, and revolving about a fixed axis passing through the centre of gravity with a uniform angular velocity.*

5—2

73. Let XYZ be the sums of the resolved parts of all the forces which act upon any particle (xyz) of the fluid, parallel to the axes of co-ordinates, ρ' the density at that point, p the pressure. Then the equation of fluid equilibrium is

$$\frac{dp}{\rho} = Xdx + Ydy + Zdz.$$

At the surface, and also throughout any internal stratum of equal pressure and therefore of equal density, in passing from point to point $dp = 0$.

Hence $Xdx + Ydy + Zdz = 0$

is the differential equation to the exterior surface and to the surfaces of all the internal strata; the particular value assigned to the constant after integration determining to which surface the integral belongs.

The following property belongs to all these surfaces. If ds be the element of any curve drawn on the surface through (xyz), and R be the resultant of XYZ; then the equation may be written

$$\frac{X}{R}\frac{dx}{ds} + \frac{Y}{R}\frac{dy}{ds} + \frac{Z}{R}\frac{dz}{ds} = 0,$$

which shows that the resultant force is at right angles to any line in the surface, and therefore to the surface itself at the point (xyz).

The equilibrium will be the same if we suppose the rotatory motion not to exist, but apply to each particle a force equal to the centrifugal force caused by the rotation. The forces then acting on the fluid will be the centrifugal force and the mutual attraction of the parts of the fluid. Let V be the potential Art. 18) for this mass, then

$$-\frac{dV}{dx}, \quad -\frac{dV}{dy}, \quad -\frac{dV}{dz}$$

are the attractions parallel to the three axes tending towards the origin of co-ordinates. Let w be the angular velocity of rotation about the axis of z, taken as the fixed axis; $w^2.x$ and $w^2.y$ will be the centrifugal force at the point (xyz). Then the differential equation to the surface and the strata becomes

$$0 = \left(\frac{dV}{dx} + w^2x\right) dx + \left(\frac{dV}{dy} + w^2y\right) dy + \frac{dV}{dz} dz,$$

or constant $= V + \dfrac{w^2}{2}(x^2 + y^2).$

Let r be the distance of the point (xyz) from the origin, and θ the angle r makes with the axis of z, and $\cos\theta = \mu$: then $x^2 + y^2 = r^2 \sin^2\theta = (1 - \mu^2) r^2$. Also let m be the ratio of the centrifugal force at the equator to gravity at the equator $\left(\text{or } \dfrac{1}{289}\right)$; let a' be the mean radius of the stratum through (xyz); a the radius of the equator; then

$$m = w^2 a \div \frac{M}{a^2} = \frac{w^2 a^3}{M},$$

and $M = 4\pi \displaystyle\int_0^a \rho' a'^2 da' = \dfrac{4}{3}\pi\phi(a)$ suppose,

the strata being considered spherical because of the smallness of the numerator in the value of m;

$$\therefore\ m = \frac{3w^2 a^3}{4\pi\phi(a)}, \quad \therefore\ w^2 = \frac{4\pi}{3}m\frac{\phi(a)}{a^3},$$

and the equation becomes

$$\text{constant} = V + \frac{2\pi}{3}m\frac{\phi(a)}{a^3}(1 - \mu^2)r^2$$

$$= V + \frac{4\pi}{9}m\frac{\phi(a)}{a^3}r^2 + \frac{2\pi}{3}m\frac{\phi(a)}{a^3}\left(\frac{1}{3} - \mu^2\right)r^2,$$

this arrangement being made, because the second and third terms as they now stand, are Laplace's Functions of the order 0 and 2. (See Art. 39, Ex. 1.)

Now since the mass is supposed to be fluid and the external surface nearly spherical, it follows that as the heavier parts, which are all free to move, will sink through the lighter, and lie in layers, these layers will also be nearly spherical, otherwise there will be a greater pressure on one part than on another, and the equilibrium of the layer or stratum will not exist. We may therefore assume as a consequence of the fluidity and the form of the surface that the strata also are nearly spherical.

By Art. 46, we have

$$V = \frac{4\pi}{r} \int_0^a \rho' \left\{ a'^2 + \frac{d}{da'} \left(\frac{a'^4}{3r} Y_2' + \dots + \frac{a''^{i+2}}{(2i+1)r^i} Y_i' + \dots \right) \right\} da'$$

$$+ 4\pi \int_a^b \rho' \left\{ a' + \frac{d}{da'} \left(\frac{a'r}{3} Y_2' + \dots + \frac{r^i}{(2i+1)a''^{i-1}} Y_i' + \dots \right) \right\} da'.$$

In this put

$$r = a(1 + Y_2 + \dots Y_i + \dots) \text{ and } \int_0^a \rho' a'^n da' = \phi(a),$$

as before. Then substitute this value of V in the equation to the strata and equate terms of the order i. (See Art. 35.)

The constant parts give

$$\int \frac{dp}{\rho} = \frac{4\pi}{3} \frac{\phi(a)}{a} + 4\pi \int_a^b \rho' a' da' + \frac{4\pi}{9} ma^2 \frac{\phi(s)}{s^3},$$

and the terms of the order i give

$$\frac{\phi(a)}{3a} Y_i - \frac{1}{(2i+1) a^{i+1}} \int_0^a \rho' \frac{d}{da'} (a''^{i+2} Y_i') da'$$

$$- \frac{a^i}{2i+1} \int_a^b \rho' \frac{d}{da'} \left(\frac{Y_i'}{a''^{i-1}} \right) da' = 0,$$

except when $i = 2$, in which case the second side is

$$\frac{m}{6} \frac{a^2 \phi(s)}{s^3} \left(\frac{1}{3} - \mu^2 \right).$$

By this equation Y_i is to be calculated, and then the form of the stratum of which the mean radius is a is known by the formula

$$r = a(1 + Y_1 + Y_2 + \ldots + Y_i + \ldots).$$

PROP.   *To prove that $Y_i = 0$, excepting the case of $i = 2$.*

74.   Since Y_i and ρ are functions of a, they may be expanded into ascending series of the form

$$Y_i = Wa^s + \ldots, \quad \rho = D + D'a^n + \ldots,$$

where D is the density at the centre of the earth, and is as well as W and D' independent of a: s, n ... must not be negative, otherwise Y_i and ρ would be infinite at the centre.

Now when these and the corresponding series obtained by putting a' for a, are substituted in the equation of the strata in the last Article, and the first side arranged in powers of a, the various coefficients ought to vanish; excepting when $i = 2$, because then the second side is not zero.   We shall therefore substitute these series, and search for values of W and s which satisfy the condition.

$$\phi(a) = 3 \int_0^a \rho' a'^n da' = Da^3 + \frac{3D'}{n+3}a^{n+3} + \ldots$$

After two easy integrations the equation of the strata becomes

$$WD\left(\frac{1}{3}a^{s+3} - \frac{a^{s+i+3}}{2i+1}a^i\right) + \ldots = 0.$$

No value of s will cause these terms to vanish.   The only apparent case is when $i = 1$, for then by putting $s = i - 2$ the part in the brackets vanishes: but in this particular case $s = -1$, and is negative and therefore inadmissible.

Hence the only way of satisfying the condition is by putting $W = 0$; this shows that Y_i has no first term, that is, that it has no term at all and is therefore zero.

PROP.   *To find the value of Y_2, and to prove that the strata are all spheroidal, concentric and with a common axis.*

75. The equation for calculating Y_2 is, by Art. 73,

$$\frac{\phi(a)}{3a} Y_2 - \frac{1}{5a^2}\int_0^a \rho' \frac{d}{da'}(a'^3 Y_2')\, da' - \frac{a^3}{5}\int_a^* \rho' \frac{dY_2'}{da'}\, da'$$

$$= \frac{m}{6} \frac{a^2\phi(a)}{a^2}\left(\frac{1}{3} - \mu^2\right).$$

Suppose Y_2 (and similarly Y_2') is expanded in a series of powers of $\frac{1}{3} - \mu^2$ with indeterminate coefficients to be ascertained by the condition, that they shall satisfy the above equation. These coefficients will be functions of a only, as it is clear from the right-hand side of the equation that ω does not enter into the value of Y_2; and Y_2 consists of only one term, that involving the simple power of $\frac{1}{3} - \mu^2$. Let it be $\epsilon\left(\frac{1}{3} - \mu^2\right)$, ϵ being a small quantity of the order of m. Hence

$$r = a\left[1 + \epsilon\left(\tfrac{1}{3} - \mu^2\right)\right], \quad \mu = \sin(\text{latitude}) = \sin l$$

$$= a\left(1 - \tfrac{2}{3}\epsilon\right)\left(1 + \epsilon\cos^2 l\right), \text{ since } \epsilon \text{ is small.}$$

This is the equation to a spheroid from the centre, ϵ being the ellipticity.   The axis-minor coincides with the axis of revolution of the whole mass. Hence the strata are concentric spheroids, the minor-axes of which coincide with the axis of revolution of the whole mass.

PROP. *To obtain an approximate law of the density of the strata.*

76. By Art. 73 we have the following equation for calculating the pressure on the stratum of which the radius is a, neglecting the small term,

$$\int_0^a \frac{1}{\rho'} \frac{dp}{da'}\, da' = \frac{4\pi}{3} \frac{\phi(a)}{a} + 4\pi\int_a^* \rho'a'\, da'.$$

Laplace has integrated this equation on the supposition that the change in pressure in descending through the strata varies as the change in the square of the density (*Mémoires de l'Institut*, Tom. III. p. 496). This law of compression differs from that of elastic fluids, in which the change in pressure varies as the change in density. The law used by

Laplace is à *priori* more probably true than the law of compression of elastic fluids, for the greater the density of tenacious and semi-fluid masses the greater must be the increase of pressure to produce a given increase of density. See also some remarks on this subject by Professor Challis in the *Phil. Mag.* Vol. XXXVIII. The approximate truth of this law is, however, shown by the accuracy of the results to which it leads us.

Putting, then, $dp = \frac{1}{2} kd \cdot \rho^n$, k being a constant,

$$\int_0^a \frac{1}{\rho'} \frac{dp'}{da'} da' = k \left(\rho + \text{constant} \right);$$

$$\therefore ka \left(\rho + \text{const.} \right) = 4\pi \int_0^a \rho' a'^n da' + 4\pi a \int_a^b \rho' a' da',$$

since $\phi(a) = 3 \int_0^a \rho' a'^n da'$. Differentiate* with respect to a;

$$\therefore k \left(\frac{d \cdot \rho a}{da} + \text{const.} \right) = 4\pi \rho a^2 + 4\pi \int_a^b \rho' a' da' - 4\pi \rho a^2 = 4\pi \int_a^b \rho' a' da';$$

$$\therefore \frac{d^2 \cdot \rho a}{da^2} + q^2 \cdot \rho a = 0, \text{ putting } \frac{4\pi}{k} = q^2;$$

$$\therefore \rho a = Q \sin (qa + B); \quad \therefore \rho = \frac{Q}{a} \sin (qa + B).$$

When $a = 0$, $\rho = \dfrac{Q \sin B}{0}$; $\therefore B = 0$, otherwise ρ would be infinite at the centre, which cannot be;

$$\therefore \rho = \frac{Q}{a} \sin qa,$$

Q and q being unknown constants.

---

* In order to explain how to differentiate a definite integral with respect to a quantity involved in the limits, let $\int f(x) = F(x) + \text{const.}$;

$$\therefore \int_b^a f(x)\, dx = F(a) - F(b);$$

$$\therefore \frac{d}{da} \int_b^a f(x)\, dx = \frac{dF(a)}{da} = f(a); \quad \frac{d}{db} \int_b^a f(x)\, dx = -\frac{dF(b)}{db} = -f(b).$$

Prop.   *To obtain an equation for calculating the ellipticity of the strata.*

77.   Substitute $s\left(\frac{1}{3}-\mu^2\right)$ for Y_s and $s'\left(\frac{1}{3}-\mu^2\right)$ for Y_s' in the equation of the last Proposition but one, and we have, after dividing by $\frac{1}{3}-\mu^2$,

$$\frac{\phi(a)}{3a}\,s-\frac{1}{5a^2}\int_0^a\rho'\frac{d}{da'}\left(a'^5 s'\right)da'-\frac{a'}{5}\int_a^s\rho'\frac{ds'}{da'}\,da'=\frac{m}{6}\,\frac{a^3\phi(a)}{s^2}\,.$$

Divide both sides by a^3, and differentiate with respect to a; then multiply by a^5, and differentiate again, and divide by the coefficient of $\dfrac{d^2 s}{da^2}$;

$$\therefore\frac{d^2 s}{da^2}+\frac{6\rho a^3}{\phi(a)}\frac{ds}{da}-\left\{1-\frac{\rho a^3}{\phi(a)}\right\}\frac{6s}{a^2}=0.$$

This may be put into another form. Multiply by $\phi(a)$, then

$$\frac{d}{da}\left\{\phi(a)\frac{ds}{da}\right\}+\frac{d}{da}\left[3\rho a^3 s\right]=\frac{6}{a^2}\,\phi(a)\,s+3a^3 s\frac{d\rho}{da}\,;$$

or $\dfrac{d^2}{da^2}\left[\phi(a)\,s\right]=\dfrac{6}{a^2}\,\phi(a)\,s+3a^3 s\dfrac{d\rho}{da}\,.$

Cor. 1. By putting $a=s$ in the first equation of this last Article, we have the following equation, which we shall find of use;

$$\int_0^s\rho'\frac{d}{da'}\left(a'^5 s'\right)da'=\frac{5}{3}\,s^3\phi(s)\left(e-\frac{m}{2}\right).$$

Prop.   *To find an expression for the ellipticity of the strata, with the law of density deduced in the last Proposition but one.*

78.   In the equation of last Article put $\rho=\dfrac{Q}{a}\sin qa$.

Now $\phi(a)=3\displaystyle\int_0^a\rho'a'^2 da'=3Q\left[-\frac{a}{q}\cos qa+\frac{1}{q^2}\sin qa\right].$

Also $\dfrac{d\rho}{da} = Q\left\{\dfrac{q}{a}\cos qa - \dfrac{1}{a^2}\sin qa\right\} = -\dfrac{q^2}{3a^2}\,\phi\,(a)$,

and our equation becomes

$$\frac{d^2.\,\phi\,(a)\,\iota}{da^2} + q^2.\,\phi\,(a)\,\iota = \frac{6}{a^2}\,\phi\,(a).\,\iota.$$

To integrate this put $\phi\,(a)\,\iota = \dfrac{1}{a^2}\displaystyle\int_0^a a'\int_0^{a'} a'x'da'^2$;

$$\therefore \frac{d.\,\phi\,(a)\,\iota}{da} = -\frac{2}{a^3}\int_0^a a'\int_0^{a'} a'x'da'^2 + \frac{1}{a}\int_0^a a'x'da'\,;$$

$$\therefore \frac{d^2.\,\phi\,(a)\,\iota}{da^2} = \frac{6}{a^4}\int_0^a a'\int_0^{a'} a'x'da'^2 - \frac{2}{a^3}\int_0^a a'x'da' - \frac{1}{a^2}\int_0^a a'x'da' + x\,;$$

$$\therefore x - \frac{3}{a^2}\int_0^a a'x'da' + \frac{q^2}{a}\int_0^a a'\int_0^a a'x'da'^2 = 0.$$

Multiply by a^2 and differentiate;

$$\therefore a^2\frac{dx}{da} + 2ax - 3ax + q^2a\int_0^a a'x'da' = 0.$$

Divide by a and differentiate, and then divide by a;

$$\frac{d^2x}{da^2} + q^2x = 0.$$

The solution of this is

$$x + Cq^2\sin\,(qa + B) = 0,$$

C and B being independent of a;

$$\therefore \int_0^a a'x'da' = - Cqa\cos\,(qa + B) + C\sin\,(qa + B)\,;$$

$$\therefore \phi\,(a)\,\iota = \frac{1}{a^2}\left\{Ca^2\sin\,(qa + B) + \frac{2C}{q}a\cos\,(qa + B)\right.$$

$$\left. - \frac{2C}{q^2}\sin\,(qa + B) + \frac{C}{q}a\cos\,(qa + B) - \frac{C}{q^2}\sin\,(qa + B)\right\}$$

$$= C\left\{\left(1 - \frac{3}{q^2a^2}\right)\sin\,(qa + B) + \frac{3}{qa}\cos\,(qa + B)\right\}.$$

In our case $B = 0$, otherwise the ellipticity at the centre would be infinite, as is easily seen by expanding ϵ in powers of a.

Hence, if we substitute for $\phi(a)$

$$\epsilon = \frac{Cq^3}{3Q} \cdot \frac{\left(1 - \frac{3}{q^2 a^2}\right)\tan qa + \frac{3}{qa}}{\tan qa - qa}.$$

And ϵ being the ellipticity of the surface,

$$\frac{\epsilon}{\varepsilon} = \frac{\tan qa - qa}{\tan qa - qa} \cdot \frac{\left(1 - \frac{3}{q^2 a^2}\right)\tan qa + \frac{3}{qa}}{\left(1 - \frac{3}{q^2 a^2}\right)\tan qa + \frac{3}{qa}}.$$

This gives the law of decrease in the ellipticity of the strata in passing down from the surface to the centre.

By Art. 77, Cor.

$$\frac{5}{3}a^3\phi(a)\left(\epsilon - \frac{1}{2}m\right) = \int_0^a \rho' \frac{d}{da'}(a'^3\epsilon')\,da' = Q\int_0^a \frac{\sin qa'}{a'}\frac{d}{da'}(a'^3\epsilon')\,da'$$

$$= Q\left[a'^3\epsilon \sin qa + \int_0^a a'^3\epsilon'(\sin qa' - qa'\cos qa')\,da'\right] \text{ by parts.}$$

Substituting for ϵ' from the expression already found for ϵ, integrating and reducing, the integral in this expression

$$= \frac{\epsilon}{q^3}\frac{(\tan qa - qa)\sin qa}{\left(1 - \frac{3}{q^2 a^2}\right)\tan qa + \frac{3}{qa}}\left\{6q^2 a^2 - 15 - \frac{q^2 a^2 - 15qa}{\tan qa}\right\}.$$

Also $\phi(a) = \frac{3Q}{q^2}\sin qa\left(1 - \frac{qa}{\tan qa}\right)$.

Hence $\dfrac{m}{2\epsilon} =$

$$1 - \frac{q^2 a^2 - 3q^2 a^2 + \frac{3q^2 a^2}{\tan qa} + \left(1 - \frac{qa}{\tan qa}\right)\left(6q^2 a^2 - 15 - \frac{q^2 a^2 - 15qa}{\tan qa}\right)}{5\left(1 - \frac{qa}{\tan qa}\right)\left(q^2 a^2 - 3 + \frac{3qa}{\tan qa}\right)}$$

$$= \frac{2q'a^2 - q^4a^4 - \dfrac{q^2a^2}{\tan qa} - \dfrac{q^4a^4}{\tan^2 qa}}{5\left(1 - \dfrac{qa}{\tan qa}\right)\left(q^2a^2 - 3 + \dfrac{3qa}{\tan qa}\right)}.$$

Put $\dfrac{qa}{\tan qa} = 1 - z$ to facilitate the calculation;

$$\therefore \; \epsilon = \frac{5m}{2} \frac{z\,(q^2a^2 - 3z)}{-q^4a^4 + 3q^2a^2z - q^2a^2z^2} = \frac{5m}{2} \frac{1 - \dfrac{3z}{q^2a^2}}{3 - z - \dfrac{q^2a^2}{z}}.$$

When this is calculated for the surface, we shall be able to find the ellipticity of any stratum we like by the ratio of ϵ to ϵ already found above.

PROP. *To prove that the ellipticity of the strata decreases from the surface towards the centre.*

79. We assume that the density of the Earth increases from the surface to the centre. Let then $\rho = D - Ea^n + ...,$ where E is positive: and $\epsilon = A + Ba^m + ...$ Then

$$\frac{\rho a^3}{\phi\,(a)} = 1 - \frac{n}{n+3} \frac{E}{D} a^n + ... = 1 - Ha^n + ..., \; H \text{ positive.}$$

Put these in the differential equation in ϵ of Art. 77; it gives

$$B\,(m^2 + 5m)\,a^{m-2} - 6AHa^{n-2} + ... = 0.$$

Neither m nor B can equal zero, because then the second term of ϵ only merges into the first. Nor can $m = -5$, a negative quantity. Hence the first term will not vanish of itself. But we may make the first and second vanish together by putting $n = m$ and $B\,(m^2 + 5m) = 6AH$. Hence B must be positive. And therefore *near the centre* ϵ increases towards the surface.

In thus increasing, suppose it attains a *maximum*, and then decreases. At this point $\dfrac{ds}{da} = 0$; and the equation of Art. 77, already used, gives

$$\frac{d^2s}{da^2} = \left\{1 - \frac{\rho a^3}{\phi(a)}\right\} \frac{6s}{a^2} \text{ a } positive \text{ quantity.}$$

This corresponds to a *minimum*. Hence s does not attain a maximum, and therefore it continually increases from the centre to the surface. In the above we have assumed that $\phi(a)$ is greater than ρa^3. This appears

$$\because \ \phi(a) = 3\int_0^a \rho' a'^2 da' = \rho a^3 - \int_0^a a'^3 \frac{d\rho'}{da'} da',$$

and $\dfrac{d\rho'}{da'}$ is negative by hypothesis.

PROP. *To calculate the numerical value of the ellipticity of the surface in the case of the Earth.*

80. In order to do this it is necessary to find the values of qa and $\tan qa$ at the surface. Let n be the ratio of the density of the surface to the mean density of the Earth. Now the mean density

$$= \int_0^a 4\pi \rho' a'^2 da' \div \int_0^a 4\pi a'^2 da' = \frac{3Q}{a^3}\left\{-\frac{a}{q}\cos qa + \frac{1}{q^2}\sin qa\right\};$$

$$\therefore \ \frac{1}{n} = \frac{3}{q^2 a^2}\left(1 - \frac{qa}{\tan qa}\right);$$

$$\therefore \ \tan qa = \frac{3nqa}{3n - q^2 a^2}.$$

If we take the mean density double of the density at the surface (see Art. 58), then

$$\tan qa = \frac{3qa}{3 - 2q^2 a^2},$$

which is satisfied by $qa = 2.4576 = 140° 45'$. Then

$$\tan qa = -0.812, \quad s = 4.0266, \quad q^2 a^2 = 6.0398, \quad q^2 a^2 + s = 1.5.$$

Hence by the formula of last Article

$$\epsilon = \frac{5m}{2} \frac{1}{2\cdot5266} = \frac{m}{1\cdot01064}$$

$$= \frac{1}{292}, \text{ since } m = \frac{1}{289}.$$

If we take the mean density $= 2\cdot4225 \times$ the density of the surface $= 2\cdot4225 \times 2\cdot75 = 6\cdot66$, which accords very nearly with Mr Airy's determination from the Harton Experiment (*Phil. Trans.* for 1856, p. 355, where it is 6·565), the equation for finding qa is

$$\tan qa = \frac{qa}{1 - 0\cdot8075 q^2 a^2},$$

which is satisfied by $qa = 2\cdot618 = 150°$.   Then

$$\tan qa = -0\cdot57735, \quad \epsilon = 5\cdot5345, \quad q^2 a^2 = 6\cdot8539,$$

$$q^2 a^2 + \epsilon = 1\cdot2384, \quad \epsilon + q^2 a^2 = 0\cdot8075.$$

In this case

$$\epsilon = \frac{5m}{2} \frac{1\cdot4225}{3\cdot7729} = \frac{5m}{2} \frac{1}{2\cdot652} = \frac{m}{1\cdot0608}$$

$$= \frac{1}{306\cdot6}, \text{ putting } m = \frac{1}{289}.$$

81.   In the course of the last eight Articles we have developed the following conditions, which must be satisfied if the Earth has derived its present general form from being in a fluid state.   (1) The direction of gravity must everywhere be perpendicular to the surface.   (2) The form of the surface must be an oblate spheroid, with its axis coincident with the axis of revolution.   (3) An additional test, though not absolutely infallible yet invested with a large degree of probability, is that furnished by the result of Art. 80, by assuming a law of density of the strata which is of itself à *priori* very probably true, that the value of the ellipticity is not very different from $\frac{1}{300}$.   We shall see in a future Chapter that the actual measurement of the form of the Earth by means of

trigonometrical operations meets all these conditions. It is
found by measurements in widely separated countries, that an
ellipse of the kind described can be drawn in the plane of the
meridian of any place, cutting the plumb-lines at all the
stations where it is examined at right angles; and the ellipticity of this ellipse is almost exactly equal to $\frac{1}{500}$. There
are local deviations from this law, arising from local causes,
which are produced by the variations of the surface of the
Earth and probably of the interior of the solid crust also.
But the average line is this ellipse. Since the variations of
the Earth's surface, in mountains and valleys and extensive
oceans, are palpable, and must have arisen since the Earth
ceased to be fluid and assumed its general form, the fact that
deviations from this ellipse are found in the level-curve while
the average curve is still this ellipse, is rather confirmatory of
the theory of original fluidity than otherwise.

The probability of the truth of the law of density made
use of in the previous calculations is strengthened by the
value of Precession which it leads to.

PROP. *To test the law of density used above by the amount
of Precession of the Equinoxes which it leads to.*

82. The Annual Precession

$$= \frac{C-A}{C}\,\frac{3n'}{n}\cos I\left(1 + \frac{n'^2}{n^2}\,\frac{1 - \frac{3}{2}\sin^2 i}{1+\nu}\right)180°,$$

I = obliquity of the ecliptic = 23° 28' 18", i = inclination of
Moon's orbit to ecliptic = 5° 8' 50", n and n' are the mean
motions of the Earth round its axis and round the Sun, and
their ratio = 365·26, n'' the mean motion of the Moon round
the Earth = 27·32 days, ν = ratio of masses of Earth and
Moon = 75. (See *Mechanical Philosophy*, Second Edition,
Art. 470: also, changing the notation, *Airy's Tracts*, Fourth
Edition, p. 213, Arts. 36, 38.) Substituting the above quantities,

Annual Precession = $16225''·6\,\dfrac{C-A}{C}$,

where A and C are the principal moments of inertia of the mass, the latter about the axis of revolution. To find these let xyz be the co-ordinates to any element of the mass, $r\theta\omega$ be the polar co-ordinates to the same. Then the mass of this element $= -\rho r^2 d\mu d\omega dr$, $\mu = \cos\theta$. Also

$$y^2 + z^2 = r^2 \{1 - (1-\mu^2)\cos^2\omega\}$$

$$= r^2 \left[\frac{2}{3} + \left\{\frac{1}{3} - (1-\mu^2)\cos^2\omega\right\}\right],$$

$$x^2 + z^2 = r^2 \left[\frac{2}{3} + \left\{\frac{1}{3} - (1-\mu^2)\sin^2\omega\right\}\right],$$

$$x^2 + y^2 = r^2 \left\{\frac{2}{3} + \left(\frac{1}{3} - \mu^2\right)\right\}.$$

The terms are here arranged as Laplace's Functions. (See Art. 39, Ex. 4.)

$$\therefore C - A = \int_{-1}^{1}\int_{0}^{2\pi}\int_{0}^{r} \rho \left[(x^2 + y^2) - (y^2 + z^2)\right] d\mu d\omega dr$$

$$= \int_{-1}^{1}\int_{0}^{2\pi}\int_{0}^{r} \rho r^4 \left[\left(\frac{1}{3} - \mu^2\right) - \left\{\frac{1}{3} - (1-\mu^2)\cos^2\omega\right\}\right] d\mu d\omega dr.$$

Now $r =$ radius of any stratum $= a\left\{1 + s\left(\frac{1}{3} - \mu^2\right)\right\}$ (Art. 75);

$$\therefore \int_{0}^{r}\rho r^4 dr = \frac{1}{5}\int_{0}^{a}\rho\frac{d \cdot r^5}{da} da$$

$$= \frac{1}{5}\int_{0}^{a}\rho\frac{d}{da}\left[a^5\left\{1 + 5s\left(\frac{1}{3} - \mu^2\right)\right\}\right] da$$

$$= \int_{0}^{a}\rho\left\{a^4 + \frac{d \cdot a^5 s}{da}\left(\frac{1}{3} - \mu^2\right)\right\} da$$

$$= \sigma(a) + \psi(a)\left(\frac{1}{3} - \mu^2\right) \text{ suppose;}$$

$$\therefore\; C - A = \psi\,(\mathrm{a}) \int_{-1}^{1}\int_{0}^{2\pi}\left(\frac{1}{3}-\mu^2\right)\left[-\mu^2+(1-\mu^2)\cos^2\omega\right]d\mu d\omega,$$

by Art. 26,

$$= \pi\psi\,(\mathrm{a})\int_{-1}^{1}\left(\frac{1}{3}-\mu^2\right)(1-3\mu^2)\,d\mu = \frac{8\pi}{15}\,\psi\,(\mathrm{a}).$$

Also $C = \dfrac{8\pi}{3}\,\sigma\,(\mathrm{a})$, neglecting the small term $\psi\,(\mathrm{a})$.

Now $\quad \psi\,(\mathrm{a}) = \int_{0}^{a}\rho\,\dfrac{d\,.\,a'z}{da}\,da - \dfrac{5}{3}\,\mathrm{a}^2\,\phi\,(\mathrm{a})\left(\epsilon - \dfrac{m}{2}\right)$

$$= \frac{5\,Q\mathrm{a}^2}{q^3}\sin q\mathrm{a}\left(\epsilon - \frac{m}{2}\right)z,\;\; \text{by Arts. 77, 78.}$$

And putting $\rho = \dfrac{Q}{a}\sin qa$, and integrating by parts,

$$\sigma\,(\mathrm{a}) = \int_{0}^{a}\rho a^4 da = Q\int_{0}^{a}a^3\sin qa\,da$$

$$= Q\left(-\frac{\mathrm{a}^3}{q}\cos q\mathrm{a} + \frac{3\mathrm{a}^2}{q^2}\sin q\mathrm{a} + \frac{6\mathrm{a}}{q^3}\cos q\mathrm{a} - \frac{6}{q^4}\sin q\mathrm{a}\right)$$

$$= \frac{Q\mathrm{a}^3}{q}\sin q\mathrm{a}\left\{3 - \frac{6}{q^2\mathrm{a}^2} - \left(1 - \frac{6}{q^2\mathrm{a}^2}\right)\frac{q\mathrm{a}}{\tan q\mathrm{a}}\right\}.$$

Hence substituting z, as before,

$$\frac{C-A}{C} = \frac{z}{2+\left(1-\dfrac{6}{q^2\mathrm{a}^2}\right)z}\left(\epsilon - \frac{m}{2}\right).$$

Substituting for $q\mathrm{a}$, z, ϵ and m their values, this is found to $= 0\cdot00313593$.

$$\therefore\; \text{Annual Precession} = 16225''{\cdot}6 \times 0\cdot00313593$$

$$= 50''{\cdot}8.$$

The value generally assigned to the Precession, from observation, is $50''{\cdot}1$. The almost complete coincidence of the result of the theory with this observed value is a remarkable evidence in favour of the law of density we have adopted.

83. Mr Hopkins has endeavoured to ascertain how far the interior of the Earth may at present be fluid, by calculating the value of the Precession upon the supposition of the mass being a spheroidal shell of heterogeneous matter, enclosing a heterogeneous fluid mass, consisting of strata increasing according to the law we have used. In three memoirs in the *Philosophical Transactions* of 1839, 1840, and 1842, he enters upon a complete investigation of this subject. We will give the evidence upon which he rests his conclusion that the crust is very thick.

Prop. *To trace the argument drawn from Precession to show that the crust is of considerable thickness.*

84. Mr Hopkins has deduced the following formula (in which we have changed the notation to suit the present treatise),

$$\frac{P-P'}{P} = 1 - \frac{\epsilon}{\varepsilon} - \frac{\int_{\varepsilon}^{a} \rho' \frac{d.a'^{5}(\varepsilon'-\epsilon)}{da'} da'}{2\epsilon a^{3} \int_{0}^{a} \rho' a' da' + \epsilon \int_{\varepsilon}^{a} \rho' \frac{d.a'^{5}}{da'} da'},$$

where P is the precession of the equinoxes of a homogeneous spheroid of ellipticity ϵ, which by calculation $= 57''$ nearly if $\epsilon = \frac{1}{500}$; P' is the precession of the heterogeneous shell, the outer and inner ellipticities being ϵ and ε: this $= 50''\cdot 1$ by observation.

The success of the calculation depends upon a remarkable result at which he has arrived, that the precession caused by the disturbing forces in a homogeneous shell filled with homogeneous fluid, in which the ellipticities of the inner and outer surfaces are the same, is the same whatever the thickness of the shell. It is therefore the same for a spheroid solid to the centre. The formula above given is the relation of the amounts of precession in two shells, one heterogeneous and the other homogeneous; and, as the thickness is the quantity sought, neither of these amounts could be calculated, and therefore the relation expressed in the above formula would

6—2

be of no avail. But in consequence of the property that the precession of the shell, when it and the fluid are homogeneous, is the same as that of the spheroid, this difficulty is overcome ; and P can be calculated without knowing the thickness, and therefore P' will be known.

We have shown (Art. 79) that the strata decrease in ellipticity in passing downwards: hence $\epsilon' - \epsilon$ is never negative, and the fraction on the right hand in the above formula is never negative, and is never so large as unity; let it $= \beta$. Hence

$$\frac{\epsilon}{\epsilon} = \frac{7}{8} - \beta, \quad \text{or } \epsilon \text{ is less than } \frac{7}{8}\epsilon ;$$

and therefore, because the ellipticity decreases in descending, the thickness must be greater than would correspond with an ellipticity of the inner surface of the shell equal to 7-8ths of that of the outer surface.

If solidification took place solely from pressure, the surfaces of equal density would be surfaces of equal degrees of solidity. If we use the formula for finding ϵ in Art. 78, and make $qa = 150°$, and the mean density $= 2\cdot4225$ times the superficial density (the second of the values in Art. 80), then if $\epsilon = \frac{7}{8}\epsilon$ in the formula of Art. 78, we have, after reduction, $a = \frac{3}{4}a$, or the thickness equal to one fourth of the radius, or 1000 miles. If a smaller ratio of densities is used than $2\cdot4225$, the thickness is greater. (Mr Hopkins shows also that a ratio a little larger than 3 makes the thickness 1-5th of the radius: but this ratio is too large. The ratio generally used is about $2\cdot2$).

But solidification depends upon temperature, as well as upon pressure.   In his third memoir (*Phil. Trans.* 1842), Mr Hopkins shows that the isothermal surfaces increase in ellipticity in passing downwards.   If temperature alone regulated the solidification, these surfaces would be the surfaces of equal solidity. But since both pressure and temperature have their effects, the ellipticities of the surfaces of equal solidity must lie between those of the isothermal and the equi-dense surfaces. Hence the surface of equal solidity at any depth will be more elliptic than the surface of equal density at that depth : and therefore the inner surface of the solid shell, of which the ellipticity is $\frac{7}{8}\epsilon$, must be at a depth corresponding to a stratum of equal density of smaller ellipticity than $\frac{7}{8}\epsilon$, that is, at a greater depth than 1000 miles.

In the above reasoning β has been neglected. If its value be used, it strengthens the argument for a greater thickness than 1000 miles.

We may, therefore, safely conclude that 1000 miles is the least thickness of the solid crust. In the calculation it has been assumed that the transition from the solid shell to the fluid nucleus is abrupt. This will hardly be the case. The above result will therefore apply to the *effective* surface, lying near the really solid shell. But in consequence of the tendency, as shown above, of every cause being to prove that the crust is really thicker than 1000 miles, we may safely take this to be its least limit.

85. Professors Hennessy and Haughton have both written upon this subject : see *Phil. Trans.* 1851, and *Transactions of the Royal Irish Academy*, 1852. The first makes the thickness be between 18 and 600 miles. But in his calculation he assumes that the shell is so rigid as to resist, without change of form, the internal pressure which arises from the inner surface ceasing to be one of fluid equilibrium : an assumption which cannot be considered admissible. Moreover he supposes that in cooling the outer shell will contract less than the fluid nucleus ; which can hardly be true.

Mr Haughton's investigation is simply a problem of densities, and determines nothing whatever regarding the ratio of the solid to the fluid parts of the Earth. (See *Philosophical Magazine*, Sept. 1860.)

PROP. *To show what influence the present aspect of the surface of the Earth has upon the argument for the thickness of the crust.*

86. The following considerations are sufficient to show that the crust of the Earth must at the present date be very thick.

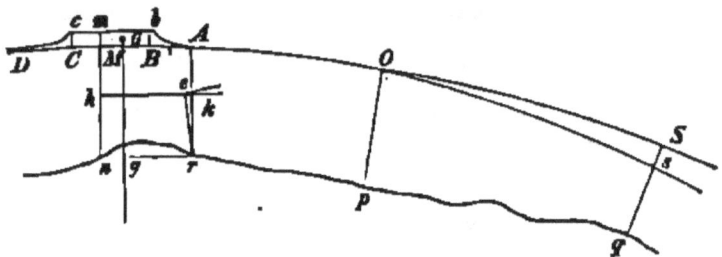

The above diagram represents a vertical meridian section of Hindostan, the Ocean, and the crust of the Earth, through O, or Cape Comorin. $AbcD$ is the average form of the mountain mass: $AB = 140$, $BC = 230$, $Bb = Cc = 2\cdot5$ miles: $mn = t$, $Ar = t'$ the thickness of the crust below m (any point on the table-land) and A: arc $AM = a$, area of $AbmM = K$; G its centre of gravity, Gg vertical; $rg = k$, perpendicular to Gg; $Mm = h$; h and k the middle points of mn and Ar; he perpendicular to mn; $re = y$, to he.

The mass Mr is held in equilibrium by its weight, the downward pressure of the overlying mass MA, the upward pressure of the fluid below, and the force of adhesion at the joints mn and Ar. Since the crust has, by hypothesis, been formed by the solidification of the fluid, its density at any point will be very much the same as the fluid was at that point. We will at present assume it to be the same. Hence the weight of $Mr =$ the upward pressure of the fluid, and the weight of MbA tends to break the crust, and is sustained by the adhesion at the joints. Let C be the length of rock, of a unit section, the weight of which equals the average force of adhesion on a unit of surface. $C = 1\text{-}5$th mile, may be considered to be the greatest limit of C (see *Phil. Trans.* 1855, p. 102).

If the point m sink, the joints Ar and mn will open at A and n, and an opening will take place at some other point on the left. The equation of moments of the forces acting on Mr taken about r is

$$K.k = C.t.y + C.t'.\tfrac{1}{2}t'$$

$$= C.t\{r - \tfrac{1}{2}t + h - (r - t')\cos a\} + \tfrac{1}{2}C.t'^{2};$$

$$\therefore 2K.k = \{t'^{2} + 2tt'\cos a - t^{2} + 2(r\text{ vers }a + h)\,t\}\,C \dots (1).$$

Take the case of m being at c, then $k = rg = 255$ miles: $a = 5^{\circ} 19'$, $\cos a = 0.9957$, r vers $a = 17.2$ miles: take $K = Cb$ (*omitting ABb*), this $= 230 \times 2.5 = 575$ square miles; $h = 2.5$;

$$\therefore t'^{2} + 2tt - t^{2} + 39.4t = 1466250 = (1212)^{2}\text{ nearly.}$$

If t be very small, $t' = 1212$ nearly; this is a condition which no law of cooling could bring about. Also t' cannot be small, otherwise t^{2} would be negative. If $t = t'$, then each is greater than 800 miles.

Formula (1) may be applied to find the least thickness of the crust beneath S, any point on the Ocean south of Cape Comorin, to prevent its bed Os being broken up by the lava from below. Make O the centre of moments: $Op = t'$, $sq = t$, $OS = a$, $Ss = -h$. Suppose that the depth of the Ocean increases uniformly with the distance from O, and is 3 miles at 25° distance from O, i. e. between Madagascar and Australia; then $h = 14\sin\tfrac{1}{2}a$. Also $K =$ area OSs; and $K.k$, the moment about O of the several elementary portions, $= 18.7r^{2}\sin^{2}\tfrac{1}{2}a$ by integration. Hence formula (1) becomes

$$t'^{2} + 2tt'\cos a - t^{2} + 2(r\text{ vers }a - 14\sin\tfrac{1}{2}a)\,t = 187r^{2}\sin^{2}\tfrac{1}{2}a.$$

If a is so taken, that the coefficient of t may be neglected,

$$\therefore t'^{2} + 2t't\cos a - t^{2} = 187r^{2}\sin^{2}\tfrac{1}{2}a.$$

As before, neither t nor t' can be small. If $t = t'$; then each $= r\sin\tfrac{1}{2}a\sqrt{93.5\sin\tfrac{1}{2}a} = 1000$ miles, when $a =$ only 10°. In this case the coefficient of $t = 118$, which may be neglected. Therefore, as before, the thickness must be very great to prevent the crust being broken through.

It has been assumed, that the density of the crust is everywhere the same as the fluid from which it was formed by solidification. Suppose, however, that it is more dense, then the tendency of the crust to break, in the first case, will be greater than we have made it, though the tendency in the second will be less. The reverse will be the case if the crust is lighter than the fluid from which it is formed. So that in any case a fracture must take place somewhere, either beneath the mountains or beneath the ocean, unless the thickness is very great. As both the mountains and the ocean-bed retain their positions of elevation and depression, we have no alternative to choose but that the thickness of the crust is very great.

87.   The result of the whole proves that the crust must be very thick: and, as Mr Hopkins's calculation appears to be free from objection, and in fact to be the only one on which any reliance can be placed, we may conclude that the thickness is at least 1000 miles.

The present form of the surface in mountains, table-lands, continents, and oceans has been, no doubt, acquired from a process of expansion and contraction which the crust has undergone during the ages since it was first consolidated. Geology teaches us that these elevations and depressions of vast regions are at this present day going on. We may, therefore, fairly conclude—especially with this evidence that the crust is so thick—that the present varieties of the Earth's contour have grown from this cause, and have not arisen in any way from the operation of hydrostatic principles.

This does not in any way contravene the hypothesis that the Earth was once a fluid mass, and has received its general figure from that condition. The fact that its mean form, as measured by geodetic operations, coincides with the fluid-form calculated upon an assumed, but (à priori) very probable, law of density, is an unanswerable argument in favour of the hypothesis of original fluidity. And the coincidence of the calculated amount of Precession, on this law of density, with its observed amount, is a very strong evidence that that law of density is the law of nature.

CHAPTER II.

88. Upon the hypothesis of the Earth being a fluid mass it was shown by Clairaut, in his celebrated work *Figure de la Terre*, published in 1743, that the increase of gravity in passing from the equator to the poles varies as the square of the sine of the latitude, and that a certain relation must necessarily subsist between the ellipticity and the amount of gravity, a relation which has been ever since known as Clairaut's Theorem. Laplace demonstrated the same, on the simpler hypothesis of the surface only being a surface of equilibrium, and the interior being solid or fluid, but consisting of strata nearly spherical. Professor Stokes, in an investigation published in the *Cambridge Philosophical Transactions* for 1849, has done the same, without making any assumption whatever regarding the constitution of the interior of the mass, but assuming only that the surface is a spheroid of equilibrium, of small ellipticity. The present Chapter is borrowed wholly from Mr Stokes's investigation. Clairaut's Theorem is valuable as it gives us the means of determining the ellipticity by means of pendulum oscillations, the times of which measure the force of gravity at the several stations where experiments are made.

PROP. *To find the law of gravity at the surface of a spheroid of equilibrium and of small ellipticity.*

89. Let V be the potential of the mass. Then because the surface is a surface of equilibrium,

$$\text{const.} = V + \tfrac{1}{2}w^2 (1 - \mu^2) r^2.$$

By a process precisely like that in Art. 23 we have, for an external point,

$$r \frac{d^2 . r V}{dr^2} + \frac{d}{d\mu} \left\{ (1 - \mu^2) \frac{dV}{d\mu} \right\} + \frac{1}{1 - \mu^2} \frac{d^2 V}{d\omega^2} = 0.$$

Let V be expanded in a series of Laplace's Functions,

$$V_0 + V_1 + \dots + V_i + \dots$$

Then since the above equation is linear with respect to V, and a series of Laplace's Functions cannot equal zero unless the Functions are separately zero (see Art. 35), we have, by substituting the above series for V and remembering the condition given by Laplace's Equation,

$$r \frac{d^2 . r V_i}{dr^2} - i (i + 1) V_i = 0;$$

$$\therefore V_i = \frac{W_i}{r^{i+1}} + Z_i r^i,$$

where W_i and Z_i are independent of r. The complete value of V becomes

$$V = \frac{W_0}{r} + \frac{W_1}{r^2} + \frac{W_2}{r^3} + \dots + Z_0 + r Z_1 + r^2 Z_2 + \dots$$

Now V evidently vanishes, from its very definition, when r is infinite. Hence $Z_0 = 0, Z_1 = 0, Z_2 = 0 \dots$

$$\therefore V = \frac{W_0}{r} + \frac{W_1}{r^2} + \frac{W_2}{r^3} + \dots$$

If the surface were spherical, this expression would be reduced to its first term. Hence in our case $W_1, W_2 \dots$ must be all small quantities of the first and higher orders.

Substituting this in the equation of equilibrium and putting

$$r = a \left\{ 1 + \epsilon \left(\frac{1}{3} - \mu^2 \right) \right\},$$

we have

$$\text{const.} = \frac{W_0}{a} \left\{ 1 - \epsilon \left(\frac{1}{3} - \mu^2 \right) \right\} + \frac{W_1}{a^2} + \frac{W_2}{a^3} + \ldots + \frac{1}{2} w^2 a^2 (1 - \mu^2).$$

Equate the sums of Laplace's Functions of the same order to zero;

$$\therefore \quad W_0 = a \, \text{const.} - \frac{1}{3} w^2 a^3, \quad W_1 = 0,$$

$$W_2 = \left(W_0 \epsilon - \frac{1}{2} w^2 a^3 \right) a^2 \left(\frac{1}{3} - \mu^2 \right),$$

$$W_3 = 0, \quad W_4 = 0 \ldots$$

$$\therefore \quad V = \frac{W_0}{r} + \left(W_0 \epsilon - \frac{1}{2} w^2 a^3 \right) \frac{a^2}{r^3} \left(\frac{1}{3} - \mu^2 \right).$$

Let g be gravity. Then since the angle between the radius vector r and the normal varies as the ellipticity and therefore its cosine must be taken $= 1$, the value of gravity is $-\dfrac{dV}{dr}$ — the part of the centrifugal force resolved along r

$$= \frac{W_0}{r^2} + 3 \left(W_0 \epsilon - \frac{1}{2} w^2 a^3 \right) \frac{a^2}{r^4} \left(\frac{1}{3} - \mu^2 \right) - w^2 r \left(\frac{2}{3} + \frac{1}{3} - \mu^2 \right).$$

Substituting for r and omitting small quantities of the second order,

$$g = \frac{W_0}{a^2} - \frac{2}{3} w^2 a + \frac{W_0 \epsilon - \frac{5}{2} w^2 a^3}{a^3} \left(\frac{1}{3} - \mu^2 \right).$$

The first portion of this is evidently the mean value of g, because if g be multiplied by an element of the surface and integrated throughout, the latter part will disappear. Let the first part be G; therefore also $w^2 . a = m . G$, since m is small;

$$\therefore g = G \left\{ 1 + \left(\epsilon - \frac{5}{2} m \right) \left(\frac{1}{3} - \mu^2 \right) \right\}$$

$$= G \left\{ 1 - \frac{1}{3} \left(\frac{5}{2} m - \epsilon \right) \right\} \left\{ 1 + \left(\frac{5}{2} m - \epsilon \right) \sin^2 (\text{latitude}) \right\}.$$

Hence the increase of gravity in passing from the equator to the poles varies as the square of the sine of the latitude; and also

$$\frac{\text{polar gravity} - \text{equatorial gravity}}{\text{equatorial gravity}} + \text{ellipticity}$$

$$= \left(\frac{5}{2} m - \epsilon \right) + \epsilon = \frac{5}{2} m$$

$$= \frac{5}{2} \times \text{ratio of centrifugal force at equator to gravity.}$$

90. This is *Clairaut's Theorem;* which is thus demonstrated by Professor Stokes without making any assumption regarding the interior of the mass. Nothing can be inferred, therefore, from any numerical value we may obtain for gravity, and therefore for the ellipticity, by pendulum experiments, regarding the Earth's mass having been originally fluid or not.

For a valuable and interesting account of pendulum experiments made in places in all latitudes, and the result regarding the Figure of the Earth, we must refer the reader to Major General Sabine's work on the subject, *Account of Experiments to determine the Figure of the Earth by means of the Pendulum vibrating Seconds in different Latitudes. London,* 1825*. The ellipticity thus deduced is $\frac{1}{288}$, rather greater than that obtained by the geodetic and other methods. In consequence of the irregularities of the surface of the Earth the experiments with pendulums need various corrections before they can be properly applied to determine the ellipticity. The principal ones depend upon the elevation of the station above the sea-level (for which Dr Young gave a formula of correction, see *Phil. Trans.* for 1819), and the excess or defect

* See also his latest remarks on the subject in the Notes to his translation of the *Cosmos,* Vol. IV. Part I.

of matter in table-lands or the sea in the neighbourhood of the station. If the station, for instance, be on a rock in an island in the midst of a sea, such as St Helena, the correction for this second disturbing cause will be different from what it would be for a station at the same elevation from the sea-level in the midst of a continent. This effect depends, as may be gathered from Art. 52, not upon the height of the station above the sea-level, but upon the excess or defect of matter however arranged. Professor Stokes has fully considered the influence of these causes of derangement in his Paper above referred to. He shows, that the effect of these corrections for the irregularities of the surface, and for the different elevations and other local circumstances of the stations where the experiments are made, is to reduce the value of the ellipticity, and make it nearer to $\frac{1}{300}$.

91. COR. 1. The investigation in the last Proposition gives, after making substitutions,

$$V = \frac{E}{r} + \left(\epsilon - \frac{m}{2}\right) \frac{E a^2}{r^3} \left(\frac{1}{3} - \mu^2\right),$$

E being the mass of the Earth. W_i is evidently equal to the mass, because as r becomes infinitely great the second term vanishes with reference to the first, and we know that in that case the value of the potential must be the mass divided by the distance.

92. COR. 2. Laplace first pointed out that the ellipticity of the Earth would have an effect upon the Moon's motion. The expression in the last Article leads to the following formula for the change in the Moon's latitude produced by this cause,

$$-\frac{n a^2}{2 h a^2} \left(\epsilon - \frac{m}{2}\right) \sin 2I \sin (nt + e),$$

where a = distance of Moon, h = mean motion of the node, n = mean motion, e = the epoch, or longitude when $t = 0$, I the obliquity of the ecliptic. (See *Mechanical Philosophy*, Second Edition, Art. 556; also, changing the notation, *Airy's Tracts*, Fourth Edition, p. 188, Art. 84.) This has been shown by Burg and others to equal $-8'' \sin (nt + e)$; also $h = 0.0040217\,n$. Hence after all reductions

$$\epsilon - \frac{m}{2} = 0.0015474, \quad \frac{m}{2} = \frac{1}{578} = 0.0017476;$$

$$\therefore \epsilon = 0.0032950 = \frac{1}{303} \text{ nearly.}$$

This method, as was the case with the pendulum experiments, only determines the ellipticity, but gives no evidence on the subject of the original fluidity of the Earth. The near agreement is remarkable.

93. The spheroidal form of the Earth's surface and the circumstance of its being a surface of equilibrium afford us more information, as Professor Stokes has shown, regarding the distribution of matter in the interior of the Earth's mass.

PROP. *To show that the centre of the Earth's mass coincides with the centre of its volume, and that the axis of rotation is one of the principal axes of the mass, as a consequence of the form of the surface being a spheroid of equilibrium.*

94. By Art. 18 we have the potential of the mass with reference to an external point (fgh), or

$$V = \iiint \frac{\rho\, dx\, dy\, dz}{[(f-x)^2 + (g-y)^2 + (h-z)^2]^{\frac{1}{2}}},$$

the integrals extending throughout the whole interior of the Earth. Let $\rho\, dx\, dy\, dz = dm$, and λ, μ, ν the direction-cosines of r the radius vector to (fgh); then $f = \lambda r$, $g = \mu r$, $h = \nu r$; and expanding the radical according to the inverse powers of r, we get

$$V = \frac{1}{r} \iiint dm + \frac{1}{r^2} \Sigma . \lambda \iiint x\, dm + \frac{1}{2r^3} \Sigma\, (3\lambda^2 - 1) \iiint x^2 dm$$

$$+ \frac{3}{r^3} \Sigma . \lambda\mu \iiint xy\, dm + ...,$$

Σ denoting the sum of the three expressions necessary to form a symmetrical function.

Comparing this with the value of V in Art. 91,

$$\iiint dm = E, \text{ and also}$$

$$\iiint x\, dm = 0, \quad \iiint y\, dm = 0, \quad \iiint z\, dm = 0 \ldots\ldots\ldots (1),$$

$$\frac{1}{2}\, \Sigma \,.\, (3\lambda^{2} - 1) \iiint x^{2}\, dm + 3\Sigma\,.\, \lambda\mu \iiint xy\, dm$$

$$= \left(\epsilon - \frac{1}{2} m\right) E\mathrm{a}^{2} \left(\frac{1}{3} - \mu^{2}\right) \ldots\ldots\ldots\ldots\ldots\ldots(2),$$

and other equations from the succeeding terms.

Equations (1) show that the centre of gravity of the mass is at the centre of the spheroid of revolution, or the centre of the volume.

With regard to equation (2) we may observe that $\lambda\mu\nu$ are tied by the relation $\lambda^{2} + \mu^{2} + \nu^{2} = 1$. If then we insert this for 1 in the equation, so as to make it symmetrical with regard to λ, μ, and ν, and equate the several coefficients, we shall obtain

$$\Sigma \,.\, \left(\lambda^{2} - \frac{1}{2}\mu^{2} - \frac{1}{2}\nu^{2}\right) \iiint x^{2}\, dm + 3\Sigma\,.\, \lambda\mu \iiint xy\, dm$$

$$= \left(\epsilon - \frac{1}{2} m\right) E\mathrm{a}^{2} \left(\frac{1}{3}\lambda^{2} + \frac{1}{3}\mu^{2} - \frac{2}{3}\nu^{2}\right),$$

which leads to

$$\iiint xy\, dm = 0, \quad \iiint yz\, dm = 0, \quad \iiint xz\, dm = 0 \ldots\ldots\ldots (3),$$

$$\left.\begin{aligned}
\iiint x^{2}\, dm - \frac{1}{2}\iiint y^{2}\, dm - \frac{1}{2}\iiint z^{2}\, dm &= \frac{1}{3}\left(\epsilon - \frac{1}{2} m\right) E\mathrm{a}^{2} \\
\iiint y^{2}\, dm - \frac{1}{2}\iiint z^{2}\, dm - \frac{1}{2}\iiint x^{2}\, dm &= \frac{1}{3}\left(\epsilon - \frac{1}{2} m\right) E\mathrm{a}^{2} \\
\iiint z^{2}\, dm - \frac{1}{2}\iiint x^{2}\, dm - \frac{1}{2}\iiint y^{2}\, dm &= -\frac{2}{3}\left(\epsilon - \frac{1}{2} m\right) E\mathrm{a}^{2}
\end{aligned}\right\} \ldots(4).$$

Equations (3) show that the co-ordinate axes are principal axes; and that therefore the axis of revolution is a principal axis.

The last three equations (4) show, first, that

$$\iiint x^2 dm = \iiint y^2 dm,$$

or, as might be anticipated, the moments of inertia about the axes of x and y, in the plane of the equator, are the same. They give also if, as before, A and C are the principal moments,

$$C - A = \iiint x^2 dm - \iiint z^2 dm = \frac{2}{3}\left(\epsilon - \frac{1}{2}\,m\right)Es^2.$$

Were we able to deduce C also, without making any hypothesis regarding the internal condition of the earth, the Precession might be obtained under the same circumstances. In that case, the agreement between the amount of precession calculated upon the assumed law of internal density and the observed value (pointed out in Art. 82) would furnish no proof of the truth of that law. But as the precession cannot be thus independently calculated, the result in Art. 82 affords a strong argument for the correctness of the law of internal density which we have adopted.

CHAPTER III.

95. In a previous Chapter we have shown that if the
Earth be considered a fluid mass the form of the surface will
be an oblate spheroid of small ellipticity, its axis coinciding
with the axis of revolution, and the surface being everywhere
at right angles to the direction of gravity; and further, that
upon assuming that the density of the strata varies according
to a certain very probable law, the ellipticity $= \frac{1}{300}$ nearly.

In this Chapter we propose to submit this to the test of
measurement, by inquiring whether an ellipse can be found
with its axis coinciding with the axis of the Earth and cutting
the plumb-line at stations along it at right angles; and whether
the ellipticity of that ellipse is $\frac{1}{300}$.

The method of doing this is as follows. A base-line, about
5 or 6 miles in length, is measured with extreme accuracy, near
the meridian, the curvature of which we are to find. By a
series of triangles this base is connected with a number of
stations in succession lying near the meridian, the angles and
sides of which are calculated or observed, as the case may be.
Thus a connexion is established between the original base and
a second base at the termination of the chain of triangles,
and the length of this second base obtained by calculation.
It is then measured, as the first was, and by a comparison of
the calculated and measured results the correctness or not of
the operations is tested. This having been satisfactorily per-
formed, the projections of the sides of the triangles on the

meridian are found, and their sum gives the length of the meridian arc between its two extremities. The latitudes of these extremities are then observed with great care, and from these data the form of the ellipse, of which the arc is a part, is found by the principles of conic sections, as we shall now show.

PROP. *To find the length of an arc of meridian in terms of the amplitude, the semi-axis major, the ellipticity (the ellipticity being small), and the middle latitude.*

96. Let l and l' be the latitudes of the extremities of the arc, m the mean of these or the middle latitude; λ the amplitude of the arc or the difference between the latitudes; $a, b,$ and ϵ the semi-axes and ellipticity; s the length of the arc, r the radius vector, and θ the angle r makes with the major axis. Then

$$\frac{1}{r^2} = \frac{\cos^2 \theta}{a^2} + \frac{\sin^2 \theta}{b^2}, \quad \tan l = \frac{a^2}{b^2} \tan \theta;$$

$$\therefore \frac{1}{r^2} = \frac{a^2 \cos^2 l + b^2 \sin^2 l}{a^4 \cos^2 l + b^4 \sin^2 l}, \text{ putting } b = a(1-\epsilon),$$

$$r = a(1 - \epsilon \sin^2 l), \text{ neglecting } \epsilon^2 \dots$$

$$\frac{dr}{dl} = -2a\epsilon \sin l \cos l, \quad \frac{d\theta}{dl} = 1 - 2\epsilon + 4\epsilon \sin^2 l;$$

$$\therefore \frac{ds}{dl} = \sqrt{r^2 \frac{d\theta^2}{dl^2} + \frac{dr^2}{dl^2}} = a(1 - 2\epsilon + 3\epsilon \sin^2 l)$$

$$= a\left(1 - \frac{1}{2}\epsilon - \frac{3}{2}\epsilon \cos 2l\right);$$

$$\therefore s = a\left\{\left(1 - \frac{1}{2}\epsilon\right)(l - l') - \frac{3}{4}\epsilon(\sin 2l - \sin 2l')\right\}$$

$$= \frac{1}{2}(a+b)\lambda - \frac{3}{2}(a-b)\sin\lambda \cos 2m.$$

97. Cor. If λ be small, not exceeding $12°$, we may put $\sin \lambda = \lambda$ in this formula; then

$$\frac{s}{\lambda} = \frac{a+b}{2} - 3\frac{a-b}{2}\cos 2m.$$

Prop. *To obtain formulæ for finding the semi-axes and ellipticity, when the lengths, amplitudes, and middle latitudes of two small arcs are known; and to ascertain what arcs are adapted to give the best results.*

98. Let $s\lambda m$, $s'\lambda'm'$ be the lengths, amplitudes, and middle latitudes;

$$\therefore \frac{s}{\lambda} = \frac{a+b}{2} - 3\frac{a-b}{2}\cos 2m, \quad \frac{s'}{\lambda'} = \frac{a+b}{2} - 3\frac{a-b}{2}\cos 2m';$$

$$\therefore \frac{a-b}{2} = \frac{1}{3}\frac{\dfrac{s}{\lambda} - \dfrac{s'}{\lambda'}}{\cos 2m' - \cos 2m}, \quad \frac{a+b}{2} = \frac{\dfrac{s}{\lambda}\cos 2m' - \dfrac{s'}{\lambda'}\cos 2m}{\cos 2m' - \cos 2m},$$

by which a and b and therefore ϵ are found.

The effect on the axes of any error in the amplitudes will be found by differentiating the above formulæ. In the denominators of the resulting expressions the quantity

$$\cos 2m - \cos 2m'$$

will appear. The errors in the axes consequent on errors in the observed amplitudes will, therefore, be least when this quantity is a maximum. Suppose one arc is chosen in the southern half of the quadrant, $\cos 2m$ is positive; then

$$2m' = 180° \text{ or } m' = 90°$$

will give the best result. Suppose one arc is in the northern half, $\cos 2m$ is negative; then $2m' = 0$ will give the best result. Hence the nearer one arc is to the pole and the other to the equator, the less will errors in the data affect the calculated form of the ellipse. This will be illustrated in the following examples.

7—2

99. Ex. 1. Compare the two parts of the Indian Arc from Kaliana (lat. 29°. 30'. 48") to Kalianpur (24°. 7 . 11"), the length being 1961157 feet, and that between Kalianpur and Damargida (18°. 3'. 15"), the length being 2202926 feet.

$$\lambda = 5°. 23'. 37'' = 19417'', \quad \lambda' = 6°. 3'. 56'' = 21836'',$$

$$2m = 53°. 37'. 59'', \quad 2m' = 42°. 10'. 26'',$$

$$\therefore \frac{1}{2}(a - b) = 54456, \quad \frac{1}{2}(a + b) = 20929789 \text{ feet},$$

$$a = 20984245, \quad b = 20875333, \quad \epsilon = \frac{1}{193}.$$

Ex. 2. Compare the two parts of the English Arc; viz. from Saxaford (60°. 49'. 39") to Clifton (53°. 27'. 30"), measuring 2692754 feet, and from Clifton to Southampton (50°. 54'. 47"), measuring 928774 feet.

$$\lambda = 7°. 22'. 9'' = 26529'', \quad \lambda' = 2°. 32'. 43'' = 9163'',$$

$$2m = 114°. 17'. 9'', \quad 2m' = 104°. 22'. 17'',$$

$$\therefore \frac{1}{2}(a - b) = 59419, \quad \frac{1}{2}(a + b) = 20863630,$$

$$a = 20923049, \quad b = 20804211, \quad \epsilon = \frac{1}{176}.$$

Ex. 3. Compare the arc between Kalianpur and Damargida with that between Clifton and Southampton.

$$\lambda = 6°. 3'. 56'', \quad \lambda' = 2°. 32'. 43'',$$

$$2m = 42°. 10'. 26'', \quad 2m' = 104°. 22'. 17'',$$

$$\therefore \frac{1}{2}(a - b) = 33094, \quad \frac{1}{2}(a + b) = 20882770,$$

$$a = 20915864, \quad b = 20849676, \quad \epsilon = \frac{1}{316}.$$

It will be seen in these examples that when the arcs compared are near each other the resulting ellipticity differs much from that deduced by the fluid theory : but when they are more distant from each other, as in the third example, the result is far more accordant. If there were no errors in the data, viz. in the observed amplitudes and measured arcs, the results ought to come out in complete accordance with each other, if the figure of the Earth be truly spheroidal; for the formulæ are sufficiently exact for this purpose.

PROP. *To explain the cause of the ellipses, determined from the several pairs of arcs, differing from each other.*

100. We have assumed, (1) that the meridian arc is an ellipse, that being the form which it would have were the Earth fluid : (2) that the plumb-line at all stations of the meridian is a normal to this ellipse. These suggest in what direction we are to look for an explanation of the discrepancies in the results.

First. It is obvious that the form of equilibrium no longer actually exists, as all the variety of hill and dale, mountain and table-land and ocean-surface, sufficiently testifies. Geology teaches the same more generally and philosophically. Extensive portions now dry land were once at the bottom of the ocean, receiving the fossil deposits and burying them in the detritus of rocks, which time wore down, to become, as they are now, the records of their own history. Changes of level must therefore have taken place on a large scale. Landmarks in Scandinavia, the temple of Serapis at Puzzuoli, the ancient and recent coral-reefs in the Pacific, as pointed out by Mr Darwin, all testify that these changes of level are still slowly going on. It has been suggested, with great probability, to be caused by the expansion and contraction of vast portions of rock in the interior of the Earth arising from variations in temperature produced by chemical changes. Whatever the cause, the fact is certain. The Earth's form can no longer be a form of fluid-equilibrium, although the average form is so.

Secondly. The plumb-line may not in all cases be perpendicular even to the mean ellipse. Local attraction is sufficient to produce material errors in the vertical, and therefore in the amplitudes determined by meridian zenith distances of stars. For instance (Art. 56), an error as great as 5" was discovered at Takal K'hera in Central India by Colonel Everest, arising from the attraction of a distant table-land. Sir Henry James has shown that a deflection of about the same amount occurs at Arthur's Seat, Edinburgh (*Phil. Trans.* 1857). We have mentioned that the attraction of the Himmalaya Mountains produces a deflection amounting to as much as 28" at the northern extremity of the Great Indian Arc (Art. 61). We have calculated elsewhere (see Art. 62 and *Phil. Trans.* for 1859) that the deficiency of matter in the vast ocean south of India causes such deflections as 6", 9", 10"·5, 19"·7 at various stations: and (Art. 63), shown that it is not improbable that extensive but slight variations of density prevail in the interior of the Earth,.the causes of which are not visible to us as mountain masses and vast oceans are, sufficient to produce errors in the plumb-line quite as great as and even greater than most of those already enumerated. These seem abundantly to account for the variety in the calculated semi-axes and ellipticities in the last Article, derived as they are from uncorrected observations.

101. Mr Airy has entered very thoroughly into a comparison (see *Figure of the Earth, Encyc. Metrop.*) of the various arcs measured in different parts of the world. He has used them according to their importance and value, as determined by the circumstances under which they were measured and observed. His result satisfactorily shows that the ellipticity of the mean spheroid is about $\frac{1}{300}$. The conditions, therefore, required for supposing the Earth to have received its present average form from having been once in a fluid state, are altogether satisfactorily fulfilled.

The same result has been obtained by another process, first used by the late M. Bessel and adopted by Captain A. Clarke, R.E. in the Volume of the *British Ordnance Survey*. This method we shall now explain, first introducing one or two propositions which we shall require for its application.

Let the form of the meridian line be such, that

$$\rho = A + 2B \cos 2l + 2C \cos 4l$$

is the radius of curvature at a point of which the latitude is l.

PROP. *To prove that if the meridian be an ellipse,*

$$6CA = 5B^2.$$

102. Let $\rho'x'y'$ be the radius of curvature and co-ordinates to a point in latitude l, in an ellipse,

$$\frac{x^2}{a^2} + \frac{y^2}{b^2} = 1, \quad e^2 = 1 - \frac{b^2}{a^2}, \quad \epsilon = 1 - \frac{b}{a},$$

$$\tan l = -\frac{dx'}{dy'}, \quad \rho' = \left(1 + \frac{dy'^2}{dx'^2}\right)^{\frac{3}{2}} \div -\frac{d^2y'}{dx'^2}.$$

From these we obtain

$$x' = a \cos l \, (1 - e^2 \sin^2 l)^{-\frac{1}{2}},$$

$$y' = a \sin l \, (1 - e^2) \, (1 - e^2 \sin^2 l)^{-\frac{1}{2}},$$

$$\rho' = a \, (1 - e^2) \, (1 - e^2 \sin^2 l)^{-\frac{3}{2}}.$$

Expanding this last, neglecting e^6....

$$\rho' = a \, (1 - e^2) \left(1 + \frac{3}{2} e^2 \sin^2 l + \frac{15}{8} e^4 \sin^4 l\right)$$

$$= a \left\{ 1 - \frac{1}{4} e^2 - \frac{3}{64} e^4 - \left(\frac{3}{4} e^2 + \frac{3}{16} e^4\right) \cos 2l + \frac{15}{64} e^4 \cos 4l \right\}.$$

Comparing this with $\rho' = A + 2B \cos 2l + 2C \cos 4l$,

$$A = a \left(1 - \frac{1}{4} e^2 - \frac{3}{64} e^4\right), \quad B = -a \left(\frac{3}{8} e^2 + \frac{3}{32} e^4\right), \quad C = \frac{15}{128} a e^4;$$

$$\therefore \; 6CA = \frac{45}{64} e^4 a^2 = \frac{45}{64} \frac{64}{9} B^2 = 5B^2.$$

103.   Cor.   The expansions of x' and y' are as follows :—

$$x'=a\left\{\left(1+\frac{1}{8}e^{2}+\frac{3}{64}e^{4}\right)\cos l-\left(\frac{1}{8}e^{2}+\frac{9}{128}e^{4}\right)\cos 3l+\frac{3}{128}e^{4}\cos 5l\right\},$$

$$y'=a\left\{\left(1-\frac{5}{8}e^{2}-\frac{9}{64}e^{4}\right)\sin l-\left(\frac{1}{8}e^{2}-\frac{1}{128}e^{4}\right)\sin 3l+\frac{3}{128}e^{4}\sin 5l\right\}.$$

Prop. *To find an expression for measuring the departure of the curve of the meridian from an ellipse at any point, when the meridian is not elliptical.*

104.   Let xy be the co-ordinates to any point of which l is the latitude, and the radius of curvature as above.

Now $\cot l=-\dfrac{dy}{dx}$, $\therefore \dfrac{d^{2}y}{dx^{2}}=\operatorname{cosec}^{2}l\,\dfrac{dl}{dx}$;

$$\therefore \frac{dx}{dl}=-\rho\sin l,\quad\text{and}\quad\frac{dy}{dl}=\rho\cos l;$$

$$\therefore x=(A-B)\cos l+\frac{1}{3}(B-C)\cos 3l+\frac{1}{5}C\cos 5l,$$

$$y=(A+B)\sin l+\frac{1}{3}(B+C)\sin 3l+\frac{1}{5}C\sin 5l.$$

Let a and b be the semi-axes of the curve, whether it be an ellipse or not. Hence these values of x and y give

$$a=A-B+\frac{1}{3}(B-C)+\frac{1}{5}C=A-\frac{2}{3}B-\frac{2}{15}C,$$

$$b=A+B-\frac{1}{3}(B+C)+\frac{1}{5}C=A+\frac{2}{3}B-\frac{2}{15}C,$$

$$e^{2}=1-\frac{b^{2}}{a^{2}}=-\frac{8}{3}\frac{B}{A}\left(1+\frac{4}{3}\frac{B}{A}\right),\text{ neglecting }B\,.\,C\text{ \&c.}$$

If we put these for a and e^{2} in the expressions for x' and y' in Art. 103, we shall have the co-ordinates of a point (latitude l) in the ellipse constructed upon the same axes as those of the actual curve. After reduction, we get

$$x' = \left(A - B - \frac{2}{15}C + \frac{1}{9}\frac{B^2}{A}\right)\cos l + \left(\frac{1}{3}B - \frac{5}{18}\frac{B^2}{A}\right)\cos 3l + \frac{1}{6}\frac{B^2}{A}\cos 5l,$$

$$y' = \left(A + B - \frac{2}{15}C + \frac{1}{9}\frac{B^2}{A}\right)\sin l + \left(\frac{1}{3}B - \frac{5}{18}\frac{B^2}{A}\right)\sin 3l + \frac{1}{6}\frac{B^2}{A}\sin 5l;$$

$$\therefore\ x - x' = \left(C - \frac{5}{6}\frac{B^2}{A}\right)\left(\frac{2}{15}\cos l - \frac{1}{3}\cos 3l + \frac{1}{5}\cos 5l\right),$$

$$y - y' = \left(C - \frac{5}{6}\frac{B^2}{A}\right)\left(\frac{2}{15}\sin l + \frac{1}{3}\sin 3l + \frac{1}{5}\sin 5l\right).$$

Let δs and δr be the distances between the points (xy) and $(x'y')$ measured along the arc of the ellipse and the normal;

$$\therefore\ \delta s = -(x - x')\sin l + (y - y')\cos l = \frac{8}{15}\left(C - \frac{5}{6}\frac{B^2}{A}\right)\sin 4l,$$

$$\delta r = (x - x')\cos l + (y - y')\sin l = \frac{4}{15}\left(C - \frac{5}{6}\frac{B^2}{A}\right)\sin^2 2l.$$

PROP. *To obtain a formula for correcting the amplitude of an arc, so as to make its measured length accord with a given curve.*

105. Let s be the length of the arc and ρ the radius of curvature as before; then, by integration,

$$s = Al + B\sin 2l + \tfrac{1}{2}C\sin 4l + \text{constant.}$$

Let $l - \tfrac{1}{2}\phi,\ l + \tfrac{1}{2}\phi$ be the limits of s, l being the latitude of the middle point, and ϕ the amplitude of the arc;

$$\therefore\ s = A\phi + 2B\cos 2l\sin\phi + C\cos 4l\sin 2\phi.$$

Suppose now that $x_{\prime}x_{\prime}'$ are the small corrections which must be applied to the *observed* latitudes, $l - \tfrac{1}{2}\phi,\ l + \tfrac{1}{2}\phi$, to make them accord with the measured length s. Then $l - \tfrac{1}{2}\phi + x_{\prime}$ and $l + \tfrac{1}{2}\phi + x_{\prime}'$ and $\phi + x_{\prime}' - x_{\prime}$ must be put instead of

$l - \frac{1}{2}\phi$, $l + \frac{1}{2}\phi$, and ϕ in the above formula. Hence, neglecting the squares of small quantities,

$$s = A \, (\phi + x_i' - x_i) + 2B \cos 2l \, \{\sin \phi + (x_i' - x_i) \cos \phi\}$$

$$+ \, C \cos 4l \, \{\sin 2\phi + 2 \, (x_i' - x_i) \cos 2\phi\};$$

$$\therefore \; (x_i' - x_i) \, (A + 2B \cos \phi \cos 2l)$$

$$= s - A\phi - 2B \cos 2l \sin \phi - C \cos 4l \sin 2\phi.$$

Put $A + 2B \cos \phi \cos 2l = A + \mu;$

$$\therefore \; x_i' - x_i = \left(\frac{s}{A} - \phi\right)\mu - \frac{2B\mu}{A} \sin \phi \cos 2l - \frac{C\mu}{A} \sin 2\phi \cos 4l.$$

Let $$\frac{1}{A} = \frac{1}{2089000}\left(1 + \frac{U}{10000}\right)$$

$$-\frac{2B}{A} = \frac{1}{200} + \frac{V}{10000}, \quad -\frac{C}{A} = \frac{Z}{10000},$$

and the above formula will become

$$x_i' = m + aU + \beta V + \gamma Z + x_i,$$

where m, a, β, γ are functions of the observed latitudes, the measured length, and numerical quantities only.

106. As an example which the student may work out for himself, the following is selected from the Volume of the *Ordnance Survey*.

Station.	Observed		Measured Arc in feet.
	Latitudes.	Amplitudes.	
Damargida	18° 3′ 15″·292	....	....
Kalianpur	24 7 11 ·262	6° 3′55″·970	2202904·7
Kaliana	29 30 48 ·322	11 27 33 ·030	4164042·7

If x_i be the correction for Damargida, then the formula, when the numbers are substituted, will give these corrections:

For Kalianpur...$- 4\cdot063 + 2\cdot1831\,U + 1\cdot6212\,V + 0\cdot4285\,Z + x_i$,

... Kaliana......$+ 0\cdot365 + 4\cdot1251\,U + 2\cdot7741\,V - 0\cdot7213\,Z + x_i$.

Also $\quad\quad \delta r = -29\cdot01 - 1\cdot16\,V - 557\cdot07\,Z$ feet.

PROP. *To explain the process by which the mean figure of the earth is obtained from the observed latitudes and the measured arcs by the Principle of Least Squares.*

107. Suppose that we have a number of equations with numerical coefficients connecting a number of unknown quantities, less in number than the equations; if the equations are true, the same values should come out whichever of the equations we use in the process of elimination. In Physical Science it often happens that we have a problem of this sort, in which the numerical coefficients, being obtained from observations, are not exact, but only approximate. If the correct values of the unknown quantities were substituted, they would not exactly satisfy the equations, but small residuary errors will appear, differing according to the set of equations we select for elimination. It would seem, therefore, difficult to determine which of all the results actually obtained is nearest the truth. The late Professor Gauss discovered the Principle of Least Squares, which is of eminent service in such cases of perplexity. The principle is this; that those values of the unknown quantities are nearest the truth which make the sum of the squares of the errors the least possible. In using this principle the Differential Calculus will evidently furnish us with exactly as many equations as there are unknown quantities; and the problem will be solved, with the nearest approximation to the truth attainable.

In this manner the Mean Figure of the Earth may be determined. In the Volume of the Ordnance Survey eight arcs in Europe and India, consisting of 66 subordinate portions, have been used. In each arc the errors in the latitudes of the principal stations, which divide it into its subordinate portions, are calculated, as in the last Article, in terms of

UVZ and the unknown error (as x_i) in one of the terminal stations, or in any one of the stations chosen as a starting point. The eight arcs will thus furnish 66 formulæ of correction, (similar to that for x_i' in Article 105), involving eleven unknown quantities U, V, Z, $x_1, x_2, \ldots x_9$. The nearest values of these are obtained by differentiating the sum of the squares of these corrections with respect to these unknowns and equating the results to zero. The process of calculation is very laborious.

108. In the Ordnance Volume $U = -0.6937$, $V = 1.4838$, $Z = 0.3739$; and these make

$$a = 20927197 \text{ feet}, \quad b = 20855493, \quad e = \frac{1}{292},$$

and the value of δr in Art. 104 becomes $117.5 \sin^2 2l$ feet, which shows that the greatest departure from the elliptic form is in latitude 45°, and equals 117.5 feet. The correction of the latitude of Damargida (i.e. the value of x_i in Art. 106) is $-0''.246$, and the consequent corrections for Kaliaupur and Kaliana are $-3''.576$ and $1''.643$, for the above mean values of U, V and Z. The above measures determine that curve which is nearest to the meridian, of all the curves represented by the general formula in Art. 101. It appears to be very nearly elliptical, bulging out but slightly in the middle latitudes.

PROP. *To explain the process of finding the Ellipse most nearly representing the observations.*

109. The process is precisely similar to that explained in the last Articles, C being first made equal to $5B^2 + 6A$, that the curve may be an ellipse. By Art. 105,

$$\frac{Z}{10000} = -\frac{5}{24}\left(\frac{1}{200} + \frac{V}{10000}\right), \quad \therefore \ Z = -\frac{5}{96} - \frac{V}{480}.$$

There will be only ten unknown quantities in this case. The corrections for Kaliaupur and Kaliana in terms of x_1, that for Damargida, are

$$-4''{\cdot}085 + 2''{\cdot}1831\,U + 1''{\cdot}6203\,V + x_1,$$

$$0{\cdot}403 + 4{\cdot}1251\,U + 2{\cdot}7756\,V + x_1.$$

The calculation makes $U = -0{\cdot}3856$, $V = 1{\cdot}0620$. The value of δr is zero when Z is substituted, as of course it should be. Also $a = 20926348$, $b = 20855233$, $\epsilon = \dfrac{1}{294}$. Sir Henry James takes as the final result for the mean figure of the Earth (see his Preface),

$$a = 20926500, \quad b = 20855400, \quad \epsilon = \frac{1}{294}.$$

The corrections for latitude (in the example we have taken all along) are $x_1 = 0''{\cdot}050$, for Kalianpur $-3''{\cdot}156$, and for Kaliana $1''{\cdot}810$. These are the quantities by which, according to the Principle of Least Squares, the observed latitudes must be altered to make the measured arcs accord with the mean ellipse above determined.

---

110. What has gone before leads to the determination of only the Mean Figure of the Earth. Any one meridian may possibly differ from this mean form owing to local causes, such as the rising or sinking of the surface from internal expansion and contraction of the materials of the crust, which may have taken place since the form ceased to be regulated by the laws of fluid equilibrium. Indeed the *average* result even seems to point out that some such change has occurred. For it appears in Art. 108, that the calculations in the Ordnance Survey Volume show, that there is a slight protuberance in the middle latitudes, even in the mean figure of the earth.

If there be any local deviations from the mean figure further than this, India seems to present phenomena which would suggest, that these deviations must exist there if anywhere; and in that country an extensive and well-executed Survey has been carried on, which supplies us with data. The particular case of the Indian Arc has been used for illustration in the preceding references to the Ordnance Volume, because the formulæ will now be of use in the following calculations. In India there are visible sources of error in the position of the plumb-line which ought not to be overlooked. The mountain-mass on the North, and the ocean on the South by its deficiency of matter, both tend to give the plumb-line a deviation northward and through different angles. The author has approximated to the amount of these deflections, as before stated in this Treatise. The following are the results he has obtained. (See *Phil. Trans.* 1859.)

Deflections at Damargida, Kalianpur and Kaliana are:—

Caused by the Mountains 6″·79   12″·05   27″·98
.... Ocean   10 ·44   9 ·00   6 ·18
                Totals 17 ·23   21 ·05   34 ·16

Errors in the amplitudes ... 3″·82 ... 13″·11.

If these be applied as corrections to the amplitudes in Ex. 1 of Art. 99, we have $\lambda = 5^{\circ}.23'.37'' + 13'' = 5^{\circ}.23'.50''$, $\lambda' = 6^{\circ}.3'.56'' + 4'' = 6^{\circ}.4'.0''$, and the formulæ of Art. 98 will give

$$ a = 20906792, \quad b = 20843795, \quad \epsilon = \frac{1}{332}, $$

which is nearer the mean ellipse than the uncorrected data in Ex. 1 make it.

111. Captain Clarke has suggested the following course. By the principle of least squares he finds the ellipse which differs least from the mean ellipse in form, and gives deflections of the normal from the normal of the mean ellipse most in accordance with the calculated deflections. This he has done, taking account of mountain attraction only; the effect of the ocean on the plumb-line had not then been estimated. We propose now to go through his calculation, taking account of both these visible causes of disturbance.

PROP. *To determine the ellipse which most nearly accords with the mean ellipse in form, and at the same time most nearly meets the anomalies in India arising from mountain and ocean attraction.*

112. Let l_1, l_2, l_3 be the latitudes of Damargida, Kalianpur, and Kaliana, corrected to the mean ellipse, so that (see Art. 109) the observed latitudes are $l_1 - 0''\cdot05$, $l_2 + 3''\cdot16$, and $l_3 - 1''\cdot81$. If, now, taking a general case, $l_1 + e_1$, $l_2 + e_2$, $l_3 + e_3$ are the latitudes for the three places referred to any other ellipse, then $e_1 + 0\cdot05$, $e_2 - 3\cdot16$, $e_3 - 1\cdot81$ are the corrections which must be added to the observed latitudes to make them accord with the new ellipse. Hence by Art. 109,

$$e_1 + 0\cdot05 = x_1,$$

$$e_2 - 3\cdot16 = -4\cdot085 + 2\cdot1831\,U + 1\cdot6203\,V + x_1,$$

$$e_3 + 1\cdot81 = 0\cdot403 + 4\cdot1251\,U + 2\cdot7756\,V + x_1.$$

$$\therefore\ U = -0\cdot3856 + 1\cdot8500 e_1 - 4\cdot4446 e_2 + 2\cdot5946 e_3,$$

$$V = 1\cdot0620 - 3\cdot1098 e_1 + 6\cdot6056 e_2 - 3\cdot4958 e_3.$$

Suppose that d_1, d_2, d_3 are the angles of deflection caused by the mountains and the ocean. Then the ellipse which will most nearly satisfy the Indian Arc is that which makes

$$(e_1 - d_1)^2 + (e_2 - d_2)^2 + (e_3 - d_3)^2$$

$$+ (1\cdot8500 e_1 - 4\cdot4446 e_2 + 2\cdot5946 e_3)^2$$

$$+ (-3\cdot1098 e_1 + 6\cdot6056 e_2 - 3\cdot4958 e_3)^2$$

a minimum. By differentiation, with respect to e_1, e_2, e_3, we obtain three equations, which after transformation become

$$e_1 = 0\cdot82493 d_1 + 0\cdot30087 d_2 - 0\cdot12583 d_3,$$

$$e_2 = 0\cdot30086 d_1 + 0\cdot34199 d_2 + 0\cdot35716 d_3,$$

$$e_3 = -0\cdot12584 d_1 + 0\cdot35715 d_2 + 0\cdot76873 d_3,$$

and from these we find

$$U = -0\cdot3856 - 0\cdot13760 d_1 - 0\cdot03671 d_2 + 0\cdot17432 d_3,$$

$$V = 1\cdot0620 - 0\cdot13808 d_1 + 0\cdot07484 d_2 + 0\cdot06325 d_3.$$

The values of d_1, d_2, d_3 are now to be substituted: they are $17''\cdot23$, $21''\cdot05$, $34''\cdot16$; and they make $e_1 = 16''\cdot25$, $e_2 = 24''\cdot58$, $e_3 = 31''\cdot61$; also $U = 2\cdot4255$, $V = 2\cdot4189$.

Hence the errors in the observed latitudes as affected by deflection, or $e_1 + 0''\cdot05$, $e_2 - 3''\cdot16$, $e_3 + 1''\cdot81$, are $16''\cdot30$, $21''\cdot42$, $33''\cdot42$. These are less than the deflections by the small quantities $0''\cdot93$, $-0''\cdot37$, $0''\cdot74$.

The values of U and V give the following results:—

$$a = 20919988, \quad b = 20846981, \quad \epsilon = \frac{1}{287}.$$

113. We have thus obtained three different measures of the arc in question: viz. I. That derived from a comparison of the two portions of the arc together, the amplitudes not being corrected for local attraction; II. The same comparison after the amplitudes are corrected for mountain and ocean attraction; III. The ellipse obtained by least squares, which departs least from the mean ellipse in form and at the same time gives deviations of its normals from the normals of the mean ellipse as nearly as possible equal to the calculated deflections arising from local attraction. The results are here gathered together:—

	a	b	ϵ	
Mean Ellipse	20926500 feet,	20855400,	$\dfrac{1}{294}$,	(Art. 109),
Arc I.	20984245 ,,	20875333,	$\dfrac{1}{193}$,	(Art. 99),
Arc II.	20906792 ,,	20843795,	$\dfrac{1}{332}$,	(Art. 110),
Arc III.	20919988 ,,	20846981,	$\dfrac{1}{287}$,	(Art. 112).

Let δa and δb be the excess of a and b for each of these ellipses compared with the mean.

	Arc I.	Arc II.	Arc III.
Hence	$\delta a = 10\cdot93$ miles,	$-3\cdot73$,	$-1\cdot23$,
	$\delta b = 3\cdot77$,,	$-2\cdot20$,	$-1\cdot60$.

PROP. *To find the difference in length, and also the distance at the middle latitude, of two elliptic arcs of small ellipticity, lying in the plane of the meridian, and having their extremities in the same points; the latitudes of those points being known approximately, and the ellipses to which the arcs belong having their axes parallel.*

114. Let a and β be the co-ordinates to the centre of the ellipse, of which a, b, ϵ are the semi-axes and ellipticity, measured from some fixed point near the centres of the two ellipses. The squares and products of $a - b$, ϵ, a and β will be neglected. Let s be the length of the elliptic arc between the stations, l and l' the observed (or approximate) latitudes of the extremities, λ and m the amplitude and middle latitude.

First. We will find the length of the arc. Let c be the chord, r and θ, r' and θ' the polar co-ordinates from the centre of the ellipse to the extremities of the arc.

$$\therefore c^2 = r^2 + r'^2 - 2rr' \cos(\theta - \theta') = 2rr' \{1 - \cos(\theta - \theta')\} + (r - r')^2,$$

$$r = a(1 - \epsilon \sin^2 l), \quad r' = a(1 - \epsilon \sin^2 l').$$

Also $\quad \tan \theta = (1 - 2\epsilon) \tan l, \quad \theta = l - \epsilon \sin 2l;$

$$\therefore \theta - \theta' = \lambda - 2\epsilon \sin \lambda \cos 2m;$$

$$\therefore 1 - \cos(\theta - \theta') = 1 - \cos \lambda - 2\epsilon \sin^2 \lambda \cos 2m$$

$$= 2 \sin^2 \frac{1}{2} \lambda \{1 - 2\epsilon(1 + \cos \lambda) \cos 2m\};$$

$$\therefore c^2 = 4a^2 \sin^2 \frac{1}{2} \lambda \{1 - 2\epsilon(1 + \cos \lambda) \cos 2m - \epsilon(\sin^2 l + \sin^2 l')\}$$

$$= 4a^2 \sin^2 \frac{1}{2} \lambda [1 - \epsilon \{1 + (2 + \cos \lambda) \cos 2m\}];$$

$$\therefore \sin \frac{1}{2} \lambda = \frac{c}{2a} \left[1 + \frac{1}{2} \epsilon \{1 + (2 + \cos \lambda) \cos 2m\} \right];$$

8

$$\therefore \frac{\lambda}{2} = \sin^{-1}\frac{c}{2a} + \frac{1}{2}\epsilon\left\{1 + (2 + \cos\lambda)\cos 2m\right\}\frac{c}{\sqrt{4a^2 - c^2}}$$

$$= \sin^{-1}\frac{c}{2a} + \frac{1}{2}\epsilon\left\{1 + (2 + \cos\lambda)\cos 2m\right\}\tan\frac{1}{2}\lambda.$$

Now $s = a\left(1 - \frac{1}{2}\epsilon\right)\lambda - \frac{3}{2}a\epsilon\sin\lambda\cos 2m$, by Art. 96,

$$= a(2 - \epsilon)\sin^{-1}\frac{c}{2a} + a\epsilon\left\{1 + (2 + \cos\lambda)\cos 2m\right\}\tan\frac{1}{2}\lambda$$

$$- \frac{3}{2}a\epsilon\sin\lambda\cos 2m$$

$$= (a + b)\sin^{-1}\frac{c}{2a} + (a - b)\left\{1 + \frac{1}{2}(1 - \cos\lambda)\cos 2m\right\}\tan\frac{1}{2}\lambda.$$

Taking the variations, c being constant,

$$\delta s = (\delta a + \delta b)\sin^{-1}\frac{c}{2a} - \frac{a + b}{a}\frac{c\delta a}{\sqrt{4a^2 - c^2}}$$

$$+ (\delta a - \delta b)\left\{1 + \frac{1}{2}(1 - \cos\lambda)\cos 2m\right\}\tan\frac{1}{2}\lambda.$$

The terms being small we may approximate;

$$\therefore \delta s = (\delta a + \delta b)\frac{1}{2}\lambda - 2\tan\frac{1}{2}\lambda\,.\,\delta a$$

$$+ (\delta a - \delta b)\left\{1 + \frac{1}{2}(1 - \cos\lambda)\cos 2m\right\}\tan\frac{1}{2}\lambda$$

$$= (\delta a + \delta b)\left(\frac{1}{2}\lambda - \tan\frac{1}{2}\lambda\right) + (\delta a - \delta b)\frac{1}{2}\tan\frac{1}{2}\lambda(1 - \cos\lambda)\cos 2m.$$

115. *Secondly.* The distance between the arcs.

The equation to the local ellipse is

$$\frac{(x - a)^2}{a^2} + \frac{(y - \beta)^2}{\beta^2} = 1;$$

$$\therefore\ x^2+y^2 \text{ or } r^2 = a^2 + 2ax + 2\beta y - 2\epsilon(a^2 - x^2)$$
$$= a^2 + 2a\alpha\cos\theta + 2a\beta\sin\theta - 2a^2\epsilon\sin^2\theta;$$
$$\therefore\ r = a + \alpha\cos\theta + \beta\sin\theta - a\epsilon\sin^2\theta.$$

Let R, C, C' be the values of r at the mid-latitude and at the extremities of the arc;

$$\therefore\ R = a + \alpha\cos m + \beta\sin m - (a-b)\sin^2 m,$$
$$C = a + \alpha\cos l + \beta\sin l - (a-b)\sin^2 l,$$
$$C' = a + \alpha\cos l' + \beta\sin l' - (a-b)\sin^2 l'.$$

Multiply by 1, M, and N; add, and make the coefficients of α and β vanish;

$$\therefore\ \cos m + M\cos l + N\cos l' = 0,\ \sin m + M\sin l + N\sin l' = 0;$$

$$\therefore\ M = -\frac{\sin(m-l)}{\sin(l'-l)} = -\frac{1}{2}\sec\frac{1}{2}\lambda = N;$$

$$R + MC + NC'$$
$$= a(1+M+N) - (a-b)(\sin^2 m + M\sin^2 l + N\sin^2 l')$$
$$= a(1+2M) - \frac{1}{2}(a-b)\{1 - \cos 2m + 2M(1 - \cos\lambda\cos 2m)\}$$
$$= \frac{1}{2}(a+b)(1+2M) + \frac{1}{2}(a-b)(1 + 2M\cos\lambda)\cos 2m$$
$$= \frac{1}{2}(a+b)\left(1 - \sec\frac{1}{2}\lambda\right) + \frac{1}{2}(a-b)\left(1 - \sec\frac{1}{2}\lambda\cos\lambda\right)\cos 2m.$$

Taking the variations, the distance required, or δR,

$$= \frac{1}{2}(\delta a + \delta b)\left(1 - \sec\frac{1}{2}\lambda\right)$$
$$+ \frac{1}{2}(\delta a - \delta b)\left(1 - \sec\frac{1}{2}\lambda\cos\lambda\right)\cos 2m.$$

116. In order to apply these expressions for δs and δR to the arc in question, we must put

$$\lambda = 11^\circ.27'.11'', \quad 2m = 47^\circ.34'.25'';$$

$$\therefore \quad \delta s = 0\cdot0003397 \, \delta a - 0\cdot0010097 \, \delta b,$$

$$\delta R = 0\cdot0025536 \, \delta a - 0\cdot0075756 \, \delta b.$$

Substituting the values of δa and δb, Art. 113,

	Arc I.	Arc II.	Arc III.
$\delta s =$	$- 0\cdot0000936,$	$0\cdot0009543,$	$0\cdot0001977$ miles,
$\delta R =$	$- 0\cdot0006492,$	$0\cdot0071414,$	$0\cdot0089798 \ \ldots$

These quantities are so small as to be practically insensible : the largest value of δs being 1 foot in an arc of 800 miles, and the largest value of δR being less than 12 yards.

The result is, that the differences which are found to exist, between the observed amplitudes of arcs and the same amplitudes calculated geodetically, can in no respect be accounted for by supposing the arcs to be curved differently from the mean ellipse; because, as the above calculation shows, the ellipses may differ considerably in form without producing a sensible effect upon the length of the arc. This conclusion differs from that come to in the first edition of this work. In that edition (Art. 104) the distance of one extremity of the arc from the centre of the ellipse was taken to be the same in the local and the mean ellipse; that is, those ellipses were supposed to be concentric, which they need not be, and are seen from the above investigation not to be.

PROP. *The differences between the astronomical and geodetical amplitudes of an arc of meridian arise solely from local attraction, and are an accurate measure of the differences of local attraction at the extremities of the arc.*

117. The truth of this Proposition appears from the last Article. But we will establish it further by ascertaining how great a departure from the mean ellipse may exist without its producing even 1'' of difference only in the amplitudes, as measured by the heavens and by the Earth.

By Art. 116, as $1° = 69·5$ miles,

$$0·0003397\delta a - 0·0010097\delta b = 1'' = 0·0193056;$$

$$\therefore \delta a = 56·8 + 2·97\delta b \text{ miles.}$$

The values of δa and δb which satisfy this equation and make the sum of their squares least, are $\delta a = 5$, $\delta b = -17$ miles. But this variation in b is greater even than the whole compression of the pole, which is only 13 miles, to say nothing of the value of δa in addition. It may be safely concluded, therefore, that no hypothesis regarding the *curvature* of the Indian Arc will account for the defect of $3''·791$ and the excess of $5''·236$ in the geodetic measure, which Colonel Everest found in the two arcs between Kalianpur and Damargida and between Kaliana and Kalianpur, when compared with the astronomical latitudes.

There is no other *possible* cause, but local attraction affecting the plumb-line and level. These errors, therefore, become the accurate measure of the differences of the resultant local attraction, arising from causes visible and hidden, at the extremities of the arc. The effect of the two visible causes, the mountain-mass and the ocean, taken together is very well represented (as already explained) by $3''·82$ and $13''·11$. To change these to $-3''·79$ and $5''·24$ (the values obtained by Colonel Everest from the comparison of the arc with the heavens) we must suppose some invisible cause, counteracting the effects of both the mountains and the ocean, and diminishing their combined effect in these two arcs respectively by $3''·82 + 3''·79$ or $7''·61$ and $13''·11 - 5''·24$ or $7''·87$. These quantities are nearly equal, and point to some cause existing in the crust beneath near the middle of the arc, that is, in the neighbourhood of Kalianpur. That even a slight excess of density through a large space around Kaliana is capable of producing such an effect we have shown in Art. 65. An endless variety of other hypotheses may be conceived to produce this result, e.g. a deficiency of density beneath the mountains, accompanied by a corresponding deficiency south of Damargida towards Cape Comorin and the ocean. This double hypothesis is not, however, so simple as the single hypothesis above given. Whatever may be the facts of the case, this is certain, that the difference of the local attractions in the meridian at Damargida and Kalianpur is 3″·79 south and the difference at Kalianpur and Kaliana is 5″·24 north.

PROP. *To explain what effect local attraction will have upon the mapping of a country.*

118. From what goes before it is clear that although the elliptic elements of the actual arc between two places may differ considerably from those of the mean ellipse, no sensible error will thence arise if we calculate the latitudes geodetically and with the elements of the mean ellipse.

If however the latitudes are laid down in a map from observations of the sun or stars they will be erroneous by the whole amount of deflection of the plumb-line by which the vertical and horizontal are determined. Thus in the case before us the deflections are as follows :—

	At Damargida,	Kalianpur,	Kaliana.
By mountains	6″·79	12″·05	27″·98
„ ocean	10 ·44	9 ·00	6 ·18
„ hidden cause	7 ·61	0 ·00	− 7 ·87
Total deflections	24 ·84	21 ·05	26 ·29

These angles converted into miles, at the rate of 1′ to 69·5, or 51″·8 to 1 mile, are 0·48, 0·41, 0·51 miles ; by which quantities would the stations be wrongly placed on the map. The *relative* error is largest in the upper division of the arc, and in that case is not more than 1-10th of a mile ; but the *positive* error in each case is about half a mile.

If, then, the principal places are all marked down geodetically they will be correctly placed on the map, but if other places are filled in from observations of the sun or any other heavenly body they will be out of place by the whole of the error, viz. about half a mile.

PROP. *Geodesy furnishes no evidence, in proof or disproof, of the upheaval or depression of the Earth's surface as suggested by geological phenomena.*

119. It will be observed, that the three arcs, which have been examined in Arts. 114—116, were compared, not with the mean ellipse itself, but with an ellipse equal in dimensions to the mean ellipse and with axes parallel (because the latitudes are measured in all the ellipses from the same or parallel lines). For this ellipse was so drawn as to pass through the extremities of the arc; and we have no means of knowing that the mean ellipse passes through those two points. It may lie above them or below them. We have no means of ascertaining the position of the centre of the mean ellipse. The only way of doing this is to make a geodetic measurement of the whole of one meridian from pole to pole. Till this is done we have no evidence of any particular arc lying above or below the mean, i. e. of its having been elevated or depressed. The greatest geological changes of level, therefore, are perfectly consistent with all we know by geodesy of the surface of the Earth.

120. In consequence of the inequalities of the Earth's surface, levelling operations are all referred to the SEA-LEVEL; that is, to that surface which the sea would form if allowed to percolate by canals through the continents. The sea is thus taken as the basis of our measurements; and is assumed to have a spheroidal form. But it is possible that local disturbing forces, arising from attraction, may have the effect of crowding up the waters in the direction in which the forces act, so as sensibly to alter the sea-level from the spheroidal form. This we shall proceed to examine.

PROP. *To find the effect of a small horizontal disturbing force in changing the Level of the Sea.*

121. Let U be the disturbing force and du an element of the line u along which it acts. Then $U du$ must be added to dV in the equation of fluid equilibrium of Art. 73.

$$\therefore \int \frac{dp}{\rho} = V + \frac{w^2}{2} r^2 (1 - \mu^2) + \int U du = \text{const. at the surface.}$$

Putting $w^2 = m \cdot E \div a^3$ and substituting for V (Art. 91);

$$\text{constant} = \frac{E}{r} + \left(e - \frac{m}{2} \right) \frac{E a^2}{r^3} \left(\frac{1}{3} - \mu^2 \right) + \frac{m}{2} \frac{E}{a} (1 - \mu^2) + \int U du.$$

When the small force U is neglected, $a + r = 1 + \epsilon \cdot \mu^2$. Hence, neglecting small quantities of the second order, dividing by E, multiplying by a, and transposing,

$$\frac{a}{r} = \text{constant} + \epsilon \cdot \mu^2 - \frac{a}{E}\int U du = 1 + \epsilon \cdot \mu^2 - \frac{a}{E}\int U du.$$

Now $\frac{1}{r}\frac{dr}{d\theta}$ is the tangent of the angle between r and the normal, $= \tan \psi$ suppose: and the angle through which the normal is thrown back by the force U

$$= \delta\psi = \delta \cdot \tan \psi = -\delta \cdot r \frac{d}{d\theta}\frac{1}{r} = \frac{a}{E} U \frac{du}{d\theta}.$$

Hence the element ds of the undisturbed meridian line on the surface of the sea is elevated, on the side towards which U acts, by the space

$$ds \cdot d\psi = \frac{a}{E} U \frac{du}{d\theta} ds = \frac{a^2}{E} U du = \frac{U}{g} du;$$

$\therefore$ whole elevation of the sea-level $= \frac{1}{g}\int U du,$

integrated between the limits.

122. Ex. L. The Himmalayas attract places along the coast of Hindostan with a force varying nearly inversely as the distance from a line running E.S.E. and W.N.W. through a point in latitude $33°$ and longitude $77° 42'$, and equal to $g \tan 7''$ at 1020 miles distance: (see *Phil. Trans.* 1855, p. 91, 94; also 1859, p. 793). Find the effect upon the sea-level between Cape Comorin and Karachi, which are about 1600 and 775 miles from this line, arising from this cause.

In this case $U = -g \tan 7'' (1060 + u) u$ is the distance from the line. We may take the arc for the chord. Therefore rise of sea-level from this cause

$$= 1020 \tan 7'' \log_e \frac{1600}{775} \text{ miles} = 0.0346 \times \frac{0.3148}{0.414}$$

$$= 0.025 \text{ mile} = 132 \text{ feet}.$$

Ex. 2. As the distance from the line increases the force will vary more as the inverse *square*. Suppose that to the distance 1020 miles it varies as the inverse distance, and beyond that as the inverse square. For the first we must integrate as above : thus

$$0\cdot 0346 \; \log_e \frac{1020}{775} = 0\cdot 0346 \; \frac{0\cdot 1193}{0\cdot 434} = 0\cdot 0095 \; \text{mile} = 50 \; \text{feet.}$$

For the more southern part $U = -g \tan 7'' (1020 + u)^2$, and the rise of the level

$$= 1020 \tan 7'' \left(\frac{1020}{1020} - \frac{1020}{1600} \right) = 0\cdot 0346 \times \frac{29}{80} = 0\cdot 01254 \; \text{mile} = 66 \; \text{feet.}$$

The sum of these is 116 feet, and is somewhat less than the result before obtained. We shall not be above the mark, therefore, in using the latter.

Ex. 3. If u be the distance, in linear degrees, of the parallel of any place on the west coast of Hindostan from that of Cape Comorin, then the force acting towards the north at any point of that coast, arising from the deficiency of matter in the Ocean, may be approximately represented by the following formula (see *Phil. Trans.* 1859) :

$$(0\cdot 000059556839 - 0\cdot 000002836162u + 0\cdot 000000004072u^2) g.$$

Hence at this place the sea-level is higher than at Cape Comorin, in consequence of this cause, by

$$0\cdot 000059556839u - 0\cdot 000001418081u^2 + 0\cdot 000000001357u^3.$$

Karachi is about 17° north of Cape Comorin. Hence, from this cause, the sea is higher at Karachi than at Cape Comorin by $0\cdot 00122$ of a linear degree = $0\cdot 8489$ mile = 448 feet.

Ex. 4. Suppose an attracting force resides in Kalianpur, sufficient to produce a deflection $7''\cdot 75$ at 400 miles' distance, and that the force varies inversely as the square of the distance ; find its effect on the level between Cape Comorin and Karachi.

P. A.   9

In this case the force is $g \tan 7'' \cdot 75 \, (400 \div u)^2$, u being expressed in miles;

$$\therefore \text{ rise in level} = 160000 \tan 7'' \cdot 75 \left(\frac{1}{u_1} - \frac{1}{u_0} \right) = 21 \text{ feet,}$$

u_0 and u_1 being 1125 and 643 miles, the distances of Kalianpur from Cape Comorin and Karachi.

Taking the sum of these three causes together, the increase in height of the sea-level at Karachi above that at Cape Comorin is $116 + 448 + 21 = 585$ feet. There may be also other causes which may increase or decrease this result. But it serves to illustrate to what extent local attraction may have an effect upon the standard level to which all heights are referred.

FINIS.

ERRATA.

Page 12, l. 2, for $\frac{1}{2}$ read $\frac{1}{3}$

„ 27, l. 4, insert the powers of c as in Art. 19

„ 51, l. 2, ab imo, for 12 read 21, for $\frac{h}{a}$ read $\frac{h}{a} \sin \frac{1}{2} \beta$

Cambridge Elementary Mathematical Series

FOR COLLEGES AND SCHOOLS.

I. ARITHMETIC AND ALGEBRA.

ARITHMETIC. For the use of Schools. By BARNARD SMITH, M.A. New Edition (1860). 348 pp. Answers to all the Questions. Crown 8vo. 4s. 6d.

KEY to the above. New Edition. Second Edition, containing Solutions to every Question in the latest Edition (1860). Crown 8vo. 8s. 6d.

ARITHMETIC and ALGEBRA in their PRINCIPLES and APPLICATIONS. With numerous Examples, systematically arranged. By BARNARD SMITH, M.A. Seventh Edition (1860). 696 pp. Crown 8vo. 10s. 6d.

EXERCISES IN ARITHMETIC. By BARNARD SMITH, M.A. Part I. 48 pp. (1860). 1s. Part II. 56 pp. (1860). 1s. Answers. 6d. Two Parts bound in one. 2s. Or with Answers. 2s. 6d.

ARITHMETIC IN THEORY AND PRACTICE. For Advanced Pupils. By J. BROOK SMITH, M.A. Part First. 164 pp. (1860). Crown 8vo. 3s. 6d.

A SHORT MANUAL OF ARITHMETIC. By C. W. UNDERWOOD, M.A. 96 pp. (1860). Fcp. 8vo. 2s. 6d.

ALGEBRA. For the use of COLLEGES and SCHOOLS. By I. TODHUNTER, M.A. Second Edition. Crown 8vo. 516 pp. (1860). 7s. 6d.

ELEMENTARY MATHEMATICAL SERIES.

II. TRIGONOMETRY.

INTRODUCTION to PLANE TRIGONOMETRY. For the use of Schools. By J. C. SNOWBALL, M.A. Second Edition. (1847). 8vo. 5s.

PLANE TRIGONOMETRY. For Schools and Colleges. By I. TODHUNTER, M.A. Second Edition. 279 pp. (1860). Crown 8vo. 5s.

SPHERICAL TRIGONOMETRY. For COLLEGES and SCHOOLS. By I. TODHUNTER, M.A. 112 pp. (1859). Crown 8vo. 4s. 6d.

PLANE TRIGONOMETRY. With a numerous Collection of Examples. By R. D. BEASLEY, M.A. 106 pp. (1858). Crown 8vo. 3s. 6d.

PLANE and SPHERICAL TRIGONOMETRY. With the Construction and use of Tables of Logarithms. By J. C. SNOWBALL, M.A. Ninth Edition, 240 pp. (1857). Crown 8vo. 7s. 6d.

III. MECHANICS AND HYDROSTATICS.

ELEMENTARY TREATISE on MECHANICS. With a Collection of Examples. By S. PARKINSON, B.D. Second Edition. (1861). Crown 8vo. 9s. 6d.

ELEMENTARY COURSE of MECHANICS and HYDRO-STATICS. By J. C. SNOWBALL, M.A. Fourth Edition. 110 pp. (1851). Crown 8vo. 5s.

ELEMENTARY HYDROSTATICS. With numerous Examples and Solutions. By J. B. PHEAR, M.A. Second Edition. 156 pp. (1857). Crown 8vo. 5s. 6d.

ELEMENTARY STATICS. For use in the Government Schools and Colleges in India. By G. RAWLINSON, M.A. Edited by E. STURGES, M.A. 150 pp. (1860). Crown 8vo. 4s. 6d.

MACMILLAN AND Co., Cambridge and London.

www.ingramcontent.com/pod-product-compliance
Lightning Source LLC
Chambersburg PA
CBHW020751020726
47495CB00008B/2378

* 9 7 8 3 7 4 1 1 9 2 4 0 1 *